Girl Fi...

People tried to give the tw... adversaries: two college-age... gear. The one with the blue streak... her jet-black hair was Asian American. The one with the short, spiky magenta hair was smaller, with super-pale skin.

Suddenly Magenta shoved Blue Streaks. "You know I'm right!" she shrieked. "Admit it."

"I won't admit anything," Blue Streaks screamed back. "You're just jealous!"

A crowded cable car with open sides was not the best place for a shoving match.

"Settle down, girls!" one of the conductors shouted. But the car was so crowded, I didn't think he could actually see what was happening.

"Don't make us stop this car!" the other conductor shouted. But he had to keep his hand on the brakes and his eye on traffic.

"Take that back!" Now Magenta shoved the taller Blue Streaks really hard. Blue Streaks stumbled, and her notebook went flying between Frank and me.

"My drawings!" Blue Streaks wailed.

In a flash, she climbed over the seat. Just as she was about to jump off, I grabbed her around the waist and held her back.

And watched Frank hurl himself off the cable car and into the street.

THE HARDY BOYS

UNDERCOVER BROTHERS®

#1 *Extreme Danger*

#2 *Running on Fumes*

#3 *Boardwalk Bust*

#4 *Thrill Ride*

#5 *Rocky Road*

#6 *Burned*

#7 *Operation: Survival*

#8 *Top Ten Ways to Die*

#9 *Martial Law*

#10 *Blown Away*

#11 *Hurricane Joe*

#12 *Trouble in Paradise*

#13 *The Mummy's Curse*

#14 *Hazed*

#15 *Death and Diamonds*

#16 *Bayport Buccaneers*

#17 *Murder at the Mall*

#18 *Pushed*

#19 *Foul Play*

#20 *Feeding Frenzy*

#21 *Comic Con Artist*

Super Mystery #1: *Wanted*

Super Mystery #2: *Kidnapped at the Casino*

Available from Simon & Schuster

THE HARDY BOYS

UNDERCOVER BROTHERS®

#21 **Comic Con Artist**

FRANKLIN W. DIXON

Aladdin Paperbacks
New York London Toronto Sydney

This book is a work of fiction. Any references to historical events, real people, or real locales are used fictitiously. Other names, characters, places, and incidents are the product of the author's imagination, and any resemblance to actual events or locales or persons, living or dead, is entirely coincidental.

ALADDIN PAPERBACKS
An imprint of Simon & Schuster Children's Publishing Division
1230 Avenue of the Americas, New York, NY 10020
Copyright © 2008 by Simon & Schuster, Inc.
All rights reserved, including the right of reproduction in whole or in part in any form.
THE HARDY BOYS MYSTERY STORIES and HARDY BOYS UNDER-COVER BROTHERS are registered trademarks of Simon & Schuster, Inc.
ALADDIN PAPERBACKS and related logo are registered trademarks of Simon & Schuster, Inc.
Designed by Lisa Vega
The text of this book was set in Aldine 401 BT.
Manufactured in the United States of America
First Aladdin Paperbacks edition March 2008
10 9 8 7 6 5 4 3 2 1
Library of Congress Control Number 2007932269
ISBN-13: 978-1-4169-5498-9
ISBN-10: 1-4169-5498-8

TABLE OF CONTENTS

1. Terror at the Circus 1
2. Next Stop: San Francisco 12
3. Fake-Out 21
4. Cartoon Criminal 32
5. Wild Ride 44
6. Keeping Secrets 49
7. "F" Is for Fans 54
8. A Clue! 63
9. Superhero Action! 74
10. Break-in—or Break in the Case? 82
11. Framed? 88
12. Back to School 97
13. Paper Trail 107
14. Keeping Secrets, Part Two 112
15. Monsters and Heroes 116
16. Pretty Sketchy 122
17. Swimming with Sea Lions 127

18. *Bad Odds*   140
19. *Killer Comics*   148
20. *Calling Card*   156
21. *Mayhem at the Marina*   159
22. *Men Overboard!*   165
23. *Truly Original*   168

JOE

1.

Terror at the Circus

Animals stink.

Don't get me wrong—I'm as fond of critters as the next guy. I even have a pet parrot named Playback.

Okay, maybe I shouldn't use Playback as an example of how much I love animals. He can seriously work my nerves. But dogs, horses, cats, even mice and snakes are cool. That doesn't mean they don't also sometimes smell. You can smell an elephant long before you see it.

And an elephant stood between me and the bad guy I was chasing down.

Did I mention elephants are also really big?

"Come on, Koko," I pleaded. "Just let me by."

I peered under the elephant's trunk and spotted

my brother Frank rounding the far side of the circus tent. His red wig was sliding off his head sideways and his little red nose was gone. The white makeup he wore was streaked with sweat. He was a mess.

I'm sure I didn't look any better. This whole clown getup was a bummer. Not exactly suave.

I was psyched when ATAC (that's American Teens Against Crime, to those of you not in the know) gave us the assignment to go undercover with the circus. I had imagined being a tough roustabout, a smooth trick rider, or one of those guys who balances pretty girls in the air. But no. "Apprentice Clown" was the job title given to us as our cover.

For some reason our dad, Fenton Hardy—aka the man who created ATAC—thought this was hilarious. Not that he wasn't also worried about the danger. He knows better than anyone how serious—*deadly* serious—these jobs can be. Still, he spent a lot of time laughing and making bad jokes.

He wouldn't be joking now.

Frank and I had finally figured out the identity of the madman who had been sending the threatening e-mails to the circus owner. Why a terrorist wanted to blow up a circus during a crowded matinee is anybody's guess. If you're nuts, you're nuts, right?

So now Frank and I were tailing a clown calling himself Sad Sack Simon, hoping he'd lead us to the ticking bomb. But Koko the elephant stood in my way.

I tried to squeeze through the space between Koko's ginormous front feet and the fence. He stepped forward, blocking me.

I scooted to his even more ginormous back end. He took two steps back.

"Koko!" I exclaimed, completely exasperated. "You're as stubborn as a mule!" Though, come to think of it, a mule would be a lot easier to get by.

Off to the side, out of Frank's sight, Sad Sack ducked under the tent flap. At least I hadn't lost his trail. "Frank!" I shouted. "Inside!"

Frank nodded and dashed around to the performers' entrance.

"Koko, move it!" I tried again. This was ridiculous. Worse—the performers were going to need to get into the tent. It was dangerously close to showtime. We had to disarm that bomb and catch the terrorist fast!

I noticed a group of showgirls tottering toward the tent on their high heels. They gave me an idea.

"See, there's your crush," I told the balky elephant, pointing toward Tanya. Tanya made her entrance riding on Koko. Koko acted like a lovesick pup around Tanya. A two-ton pup.

"Hey, Tanya!" I called. "Have a great show!"

Tanya looked over and gave a lukewarm smile. As a clown, I'm not exactly a babe magnet. "Thanks," she called back.

At the sound of Tanya's voice—just as I had hoped—Koko jumped into action. Well, not jumped, exactly. Plodded is more accurate. The elephant lumbered toward the girls.

"Koko!" Tanya squealed. She held out her arms to Koko.

I shook my head. I can barely get Tanya's attention. But a big, stinky elephant gets the girl's best smile.

I didn't have time to think about being beat out by a pachyderm. The moment Koko moved out of my path, I raced toward the tent and through the performers' entrance flap.

Frank stood inside with his hands on his hips. After the bright sunshine outside, the interior of the tent was dim. I blinked a few times, trying to adjust.

"Did we lose him?" I asked.

"'Fraid so," Frank said.

I scuffed the sawdust in the ring, kicking up dirt. "I can't believe I got waylaid by an elephant!"

"The best thing we can do is find that device,"

said Frank. "I saw Sad Sack climbing down from the flying trapeze platform. After that, he vanished."

"Makes sense," I said, peering up toward the tippy-top of the tent at the platform. "No one goes up there but the flyers. They're the last to perform. Sad Sack could plant the bomb and no one would disturb it."

Frank tried to run his hands through his dark hair in frustration and knocked off his wig. We both ignored it. "How are we going to keep him from setting it off?"

"The plans we saw were fairly primitive," I reminded him. "Low-tech. He's not going to use a remote."

"You're right," Frank agreed. He turned to face me, his expression grim under his smeared clown makeup. "Which means it's already set to go off."

My blood ran cold as his words sunk in. "We've got to disarm that bomb pronto. I'll bet he has it timed to explode during the opening parade!"

"I think you're right, bro," said Frank. He raced toward the ladder leading up to the trapeze platform. "We'll worry about bringing the bad guy to justice after we make sure this place doesn't blow up."

I was right behind him. Once he had climbed a few rungs, I clambered up after him.

Climbing the ladder wasn't the cinch I had expected. My stupid clown shoes kept slipping off the little rungs. Now that I was under him, I noticed that Frank was barefoot. He'd ditched his floppy clown shoes. I wished I had done the same.

After the long climb up to nearly the very top of the tent, I swung around to get my feet on the platform. Frank was already scouring the cables, the steel supports, checking under the platform.

Me? I avoided looking down.

Believe me—I'm no wimp. I've parachuted out of planes and bungee jumped, and I'm way into parasailing. So why was I freaking out about standing on a skinny little Plexiglas platform forty feet up?

Uh . . . hello? The lack of a net? It doesn't get set up until the intermission. Oh yeah, and the fact that there was probably a ticking bomb up here somewhere . . .

"Got something!"

Frank was fiddling with a small box lashed into the corner of the platform where the supports met the platform. Deviously brilliant. The bomb had been placed so that when it exploded, the flying rig would collapse. The metal structure would bring the tent down with it.

Right on top of a thousand circus lovers.

The crazed clown didn't even need a bomb that packed a lot of punch. Just enough to destroy the rig.

Frank held up the small box. "Timer is already going," he said grimly. "We have to work fast. They're going to let the audience in any minute."

I pulled my very special cell phone out of my pocket—the one I used to snap the high-def pix of the plans we had found. We needed to know exactly which wires to pull, or the whole place would go sky-high. And us along with it.

"Image coming up!" I said. I peered at the tiny screen. "It's the—"

"Give me that!"

I whirled around so fast I lost the cell phone. It flew out of my hands and dropped down forty feet to the ring.

Glad it wasn't me!

I gripped the steel pole to steady myself. Sad Sack's head rose up to the platform. My hand hit a little bag dangling from one of the supports. A little white cloud puffed out of it on contact.

Chalk! The flyers kept bags of it up here to keep their hands from slipping.

I ripped the bag down and smacked it hard into Sad Sack's face.

"Yah!" he yelped, sputtering and coughing.

Chalk dust flew everywhere. I shut my eyes and smacked him again, trying not to inhale. I wanted *him* blinded and coughing—not me!

"What do I do?" Frank shouted at me.

"Green wire!" I yelled back, even though he was only a foot away. "Pull the green wire!"

"Stop!" Sad Sack bellowed. He blindly reached out to try to grab my ankle. I slid my feet out of his reach and smacked him with the chalk bag again. Only nothing poofed out. The bag was done.

Uh-oh.

"You stupid kids!" Sad Sack clambered up onto the platform and lunged at Frank. Frank deftly hoisted himself up to the second-level platform and kicked Sad Sack in the gut.

Sad Sack grabbed a steel rung with one hand and clutched his belly with the other. He bent over, groaning and swearing.

"Come on!" cried Frank.

I pulled myself up to the higher platform. Frank had tucked the device into his clown costume and was gripping the flying trapeze bar.

I gaped at him. "You have got to be kidding," I said.

Strong fingers grabbed my ankle.

"Up, up, and away!" I shouted, kicking away Sad Sack's hand.

Frank and I each grabbed the wide bar. I took in a deep breath, and before I could change my mind, I shouted, "Now!"

We leaped off the platform.

I instantly felt a burn in my shoulders and pressure in my hands as my body dropped.

"Kick!" Frank yelled beside me.

I had put as much oomph into my jump off the platform as I could, but it still wasn't enough to make it to the other side. If we didn't pick up momentum, we'd swing right back to Sad Sack.

Or worse—come to a dead stop in the center of the ring. Forty feet up.

"One, two, three, kick out!" Frank ordered.

We kicked out, but we weren't in total synch. We kept the swing going, but didn't gain any momentum. "Again!" he shouted.

After a few tries, we were finally kicking back and forth together, gaining power and adding height to the arc of our swing.

What a total rush! Our movement created an amazing breeze that cooled my sweating face.

I almost forgot that we had a crazed clown and a ticking bomb to worry about!

"Harder!" yelled Frank. "This should do it!"

I jackknifed the center of my body as we pulled up toward the platform we'd left, then opened up sharply and pushed my hips forward to create the perfect pendulum motion that would bring us across the ring. Frank did the same.

Who knew the flying trapeze was all about physics? I'd have to pay more attention in class.

My toes felt the platform and I flung all my weight forward, releasing the bar. Man, what a burn to my poor hands! Instinctively I threw my arm behind Frank's back. We stumbled toward the steel bars at the back of the platform and held on, catching our breath.

If it hadn't been so terrifying, it would have been the best three minutes of my life!

Frank yanked the device out of his costume. "Did you see the instructions?"

I nodded. "You have to clip the green wire, and then unwind the copper that's around the red wire—in that order."

Frank pressed his lips together as he concentrated. We didn't have any wire clippers with us, so he was working the wire with his fingernails. Finally it broke in half.

"You're doing great," I said. I meant it. His hands were a lot steadier than mine at the moment!

As he unwound the tiny copper wire, I glanced back to the opposite platform. Sad Sack would have to climb all the way back down and cross the ring to get to us. I figured we'd be okay long enough to disarm the bomb.

Ping! Ping!

That was before he started shooting.

"Done!" Frank cried.

Ping!

We ducked down. We lay on our stomachs and wriggled toward the ladder.

Ping!

"That'll take too long," I said. I saw the thick rope hanging beside the ladder. It was used in a different act, but was clipped to the flying platform. "We need to take the express!"

I unclipped the rope, then wrapped it around my leg. I grabbed on tight and slid down to the ground. My hands were going to be seriously blistered after this.

We hit the sawdust running. I stooped to grab the cell phone. I didn't want it to get into the wrong hands—not with all the goodies loaded into it. Miraculously it had survived the fall. ATAC knows how to build technology.

I hit our SOS call, and within moments law enforcement swarmed into the tent.

2

Next Stop: San Francisco

"The new issue of *Fierce* is out today," Chet said. We were standing in front of Beastly, Chet's favorite comics store at the mall. "Scotty Milner is a total genius."

"He's cool," agreed Joe. "But you've got to give P. J. Rodriguez props too. His new series, *Dragon's Tooth*, is awesome."

While my brother and our friend discussed the merits of the famous comic book artists, I noticed a pretty girl staring at us. Immediately I felt a familiar tingle. Not the tingle I get that alerts me to danger. No, this was the embarrassing tingle of a blush beginning to creep across my face.

What is it about a pretty girl that gets me so tripped up? I've faced down evildoers of all types with a cool that makes me proud. But put a teen-age girl in my path and I'll fall over my own feet. Well, maybe not *literally*, but it certainly feels that way.

"Why don't we go in and check it out," I suggested, turning away from the girl. Luckily, Joe hadn't noticed her. Otherwise he'd be trying to charm her into joining us.

"Excellent." Chet and Joe turned to head into the store. I followed.

"Excuse me," a girl's voice said behind me.

I froze.

"You dropped this."

I turned around to discover the girl holding a brand-new CD out to me.

"Not mine," I said, turning away again.

"Well, hello," Joe said.

Great.

The girl took a step closer. "This is yours. Take it." Her eyes locked onto mine. But not in a flirty, *don't you want to ask me out* kind of way. It was more of a *don't be a dolt, take the stupid CD.*

It suddenly dawned on me. This wasn't a typical teenage mall rat, and that wasn't some artist's latest release. She was from ATAC, and that CD contained our next assignment.

"That was really nice of you to return it to him,"

Joe said, still trying to get a conversation started with the girl.

"Uh, yeah," the girl replied.

"So, Frank," asked Joe. "What's the CD?"

"Nothing important." I took the CD from the girl and slipped it into my jacket pocket. The girl vanished into the crowd. ATAC agents excel at that.

"You get some new tunes?" Chet asked me. "Or is it a movie?'

"Yeah, Frank, quit holding out," Joe added.

I gave my brother my best shut-up glare. "Really, it's *nothing*."

"Oh, right," Joe said, finally getting it. "So, Chet, let's check out those new comics."

Chet looked from Joe to me then back to Joe again. He knew something was up. How was I going to avoid showing him the CD? He'd probably want to play it as soon as we got back home.

Then his face brightened. "I get it, guys. It's for my birthday."

Chet's birthday! It was this weekend. I had totally forgotten about it. Luckily, he had not only given me a timely reminder—he also gave me an easy cover.

"Exactly," I said.

"You caught us," said Joe, playing along.

Chet grinned. "Don't worry. I won't spoil the surprise by trying to interrogate you."

"Thanks," Joe said, giving Chet a light punch on the arm.

"You know, maybe we should head for home," I suggested. If this was our next case, we shouldn't waste any time finding out what it was. "It's later than I realized."

"You're right," said Joe.

"But we just got here," Chet complained.

"Uh, well, Aunt Trudy was on the warpath this morning about cleaning our rooms," Joe explained.

"Yeah," I added. "She was throwing around threats like grounding us until the rooms sparkled. . . ."

"Okay, okay," said Chet. "If you don't mind, I'll hang here. I've been waiting forever for *Fierce* to come in."

"Catch you later," I called. Then we jogged out of the mall.

Up in my room I pulled the CD out of my pocket. "Comic Con Artist," I read from the side of the box.

Joe laughed. "That really could be a birthday CD for Chet."

It was true—Chet has comics fever. Even more than me or Joe. And we're pretty big fans.

I slipped the CD into the player. A montage of comic-book covers whipped across the screen. Superheroes, supervillains, comic-book characters from movies, books, and TV shows zoomed by.

"Cool!" Joe plopped in front of the screen. "There's Shyla! And the monster from *World's End*. Awesome! Check out the Maverick!"

"Get out of the way!" I ordered. "I can't see anything."

"Sheesh," Joe grumbled, scooting to the side of the TV. "Don't go ballistic."

Now the screen was filled with the image of a cover from the 1940s, introducing one of the most famous characters of all time: Trevor Knightly—aka Dark Hawk. The camera pulled back, and we could see that the cover was in a frame on an easel in an art gallery. An attractive, dark-haired woman came into view. She looked nervous—as if speaking into a camera wasn't something she was used to.

"Hello, I'm Julia Campbell," she said. "I hope you'll be able to help me. I didn't know what to do until a friend of mine who's with ATAC suggested you. It is really important that this problem be handled very discreetly."

"I wonder what happened," Joe said.

"And what it has to do with comics," I added.

Now the video moved outside, showing a neon sign flashing POPCULTURE GALLERY.

"I've just begun a business that I'm very excited about," Julia narrated. "I am half owner of the PopCulture Gallery. We sell art—paintings, lithographs, prints, you name it. But for the first time, we're going to sell original comic-book art. Well . . ." Here she gave a slightly sheepish smile. "*I* am. My partner, Jasper Scranton, isn't so into it. But I believe comic art should get the same respect and attention as other kinds of art."

"Me too," Joe said.

"Your opinion isn't the one that matters right now," I told him. "So shut it."

"Till now," Julia continued, "the artists themselves have handled the transactions—they don't usually use reps. So this is new territory. I think this is going to be huge—and I want to get a jump on the competition." She gave a little laugh.

"Only . . ." She glanced down at her hands, lacing and unlacing her fingers. She looked back up at the camera, slightly panicked. "To get attention for the gallery, I was going to auction a major piece of comic art on the last day of the upcoming convention here in San Francisco: the *Dark Hawk* cover.

There has already been publicity about it—and I've even been contacted by a number of potential buyers."

"I sense a 'but' coming," said Joe.

"But now . . . ," Julia went on.

Joe shot me a smug look. I just rolled my eyes.

"I just found out that the piece . . ." She glanced around and leaned toward the camera. "It's a forgery."

"Whoa. That's not good," Joe said.

"No joke," I agreed.

Julia's worried face was replaced by a close-up of the *Dark Hawk* cover. The forgery. Man, it was good. Right down to the fake signature in the shadow of the hawk's wings.

Julia's voice continued. "If anyone finds out, it would ruin my business before it even gets started. And not just my goal to represent comic-book art. Everything that we've ever sold would be called into question. It would destroy us. I've put everything I have into this gallery. Jasper has too. If it goes under . . ." Her voice broke and Q, our boss at ATAC, took over the narration.

"Forgery is a dangerous business," Q's voice said. *"Forgery of this skill means experience. This may only be the tip of the iceberg. You will go to San Francisco for the upcoming comic-book convention, where the piece was to*

be sold. Find the forger and bring him or her to justice. And, if possible, get the original art back."

Joe leaped into the air, pumping his fists. "Awesome! We get to check out the con!"

"*As usual, this CD will self-erase in five seconds.*" The screen went blank.

"This will practically be a vacation!" Joe cheered.

"You thought the circus gig was going to be a party too," I reminded him, "until we got there."

"Man, do you have to be such a buzz kill?" asked Joe.

Okay, he was right. I was psyched too—especially when I found the all-access passes, plane tickets, and hotel info in the sleeve of the CD.

Joe flopped onto my bed. "Uh-oh."

"Now who's the downer?" I said.

"How are we going to get by Mom? And Aunt Trudy?" Joe asked. "We've been away a lot."

"I know just how to get them both to agree," I said, turning down the volume on the CD. It was now blaring beach music—to get us into the California mood, I guessed.

"In fact," I continued, "we can kill two birds with the swoop of a single light saber."

"How do you mean?" asked Joe.

I grinned. "What would be a better birthday

present for Chet than a trip to the San Francisco ComicCon?"

Joe stood and applauded. "Pure genius," he said. "Dude, it's times like these when I'm actually proud to share your DNA."

3

Fake-Out

"This is the most amazing birthday present," Chet said for the gazillionth time. We had just arrived at our hotel in San Francisco. "You had me totally surprised."

It was a surprise to us, too—until we got the assignment from ATAC. But I wasn't going to let Chet know that his two best friends had forgotten his birthday.

"Happy to oblige," I said. "I'm psyched too!"

Okay, I knew I was on a case, but we were in San Francisco! And we were going to be at the coolest convention.

"Can we unpack later?" asked Chet. "I want to get to the convention center and register."

"While you do that, Joe and I will check out the

neighborhood around there," Frank said. "You know, so that we don't waste time once the con starts looking for places to eat."

I knew what he really had in mind was a trip to the gallery while Chet was occupied. We had discovered that the gallery was pretty close to the convention center.

"I won't be able to get you tickets for any of the signings," Chet warned.

"That's okay," I said. "I didn't bring anything to autograph."

"And our mom warned us not to go nuts buying stuff," added Frank. "She says we've run out of space already."

We left the bags where we had dropped them and left the hotel.

We decided to go for the total San Francisco experience and hopped on a cable car. The breeze coming off the bay through the open sides of the car invigorated me after our long flight.

"Hope you're not in too much of a hurry," I said to Chet. The cable car wasn't exactly the fastest mode of transport. But it was seriously cool.

Finally the cable car stopped at Powell Street, right in the heart of downtown San Francisco. A long line snaked around the spot where the cable car—with the help of the operators—would turn around and make the trip back to Fisherman's Wharf, where our hotel was.

"I guess no one ever feels they've visited San Francisco without a ride on one of the historic cable cars," Frank said, checking out the people waiting in line.

"According to the map, the convention center is just a few blocks that way." Chet pointed up and over the big stores across the street.

"We'll check out the neighborhood," I said. "It looks pretty slick."

It did. People rushed all around us, in and out of shops, down into the transit system, onto buses and onto the cable cars. The crowd was a mix of businesspeople, teenage girls shopping, and tourists wandering around. The street was packed, and it wasn't even the weekend yet.

We figured out a time and place to meet up, and Chet took off. Then Frank pulled out a big folding map.

So dorky. Couldn't he have looked up how to get to the gallery without making us look like touristy dweebs? I moved away a few feet so no one would think we were together.

I watched the cable car operators go through the elaborate routine of getting the cable car turned around. I had no idea how much strength and coordination the job took. I felt a tap on my shoulder.

"This way," said Frank, slipping the map back into his pocket.

The PopCulture Gallery was down a street just off Union Square. Little bells jangled as we entered.

What immediately caught my eye were the original sketches for the Scotty Milner detective, Frank "Fierce" Stone. "I'm really glad Milner dropped the idea of giving Frank Stone a beard," I said, studying a drawing.

"And chucked that weird hat," Frank agreed, looking at another early drawing for the hard-boiled character.

"May I help you?" I turned and saw Julia Campbell, the gallery owner, coming toward us.

She looked even younger in real life than she did on the DVD. She must have started this business right out of college.

"I'm Joe Hardy, and this is my brother Frank," I said. I knew from the way Frank stared at the floor that he found Julia attractive. I swear, some days it's hard to believe we're related.

She looked at us quizzically. "And . . . ?"

"And we're here to help you with your problem?" I hinted.

She looked confused for a moment, then her brown eyes opened wide. "You—you're with—You look so young!"

"Our mutual friends thought that would be helpful," explained Frank.

"So we'd fit in and wouldn't arouse suspicion," I added.

"Of course." Now Julia smiled—a bright and winning smile. "Thank you so much! This really could ruin me."

"We're not going to let that happen," I assured her.

Frank shot me a look that was easy to read—don't show off. But if he was going to stand there stone-faced, I had to work double hard to make sure Julia knew we were there for her.

"Come into my office," said Julia.

We followed her out of the main part of the gallery. As she led us down a hallway, I spotted a large storeroom and two offices. Julia took us into the smaller one.

In the corner stood an easel with the framed cover for the very first *Dark Hawk* cover. You could just make out the light pencil work of the original sketch under the intense black ink. This was the stage before the color was added.

I thought it looked even better in black-and-white. The whole cool/noir feel. It added to the intensity of the image.

Frank let out a low whistle. "That's a beauty."

My brother. He can whistle at a comic-book cover. But a pretty girl? Not so much.

Julia made a sour face. "It would be if it was real."

"So how did you make the discovery?" I asked, stepping up close to the picture.

"Bloggers."

"Huh?" I turned to look at her.

"I was sending out online info about the auction and found a thread about Jeff Cohen, the artist," Julia explained. "There was a detailed discussion of this cover. There were photos of it—with the artist standing beside it, so I know that was the original. I thought it would be cool to show in the catalog, so I blew it up. That's when I discovered that some of the inking in this one is wrong."

She pointed to the lightning bolts at the top of the image. "See this? In the photo of the original these weren't single lines but tiny little separate strokes."

"It must have taken forever," Frank said.

Julia nodded. "The person doing the forgery

either didn't have the original in front of him or was in a hurry. Other than that, though, it's really convincing."

"The faces are perfect," I said.

"Yeah, the things that most people would notice are expertly executed," Julia explained. "It's just the little details the forger got wrong."

"Could the dealer you bought it from have sold you a fake?" asked Frank.

Julia frowned. "Could be—but really unlikely. If he did, I would bet he had no idea. The artist originally sold it back in the seventies. Since then it's been sold and resold. And each time a certificate of authenticity came with it."

"Still . . . ," I said.

"No," she said firmly. "Reputation is everything in this business, and this dealer and I work together too often for him to pull something. And . . ." She broke off and looked really upset.

"And?" I prodded. I knew there was something more, something she didn't want to admit.

"I can't be sure that he didn't sell me the original," she confessed. "Something might have happened after I had it in my possession."

"Is that possible?" Frank asked.

Julia slumped and gazed down at the floor. She

obviously was embarrassed by what she was about to tell us.

"I didn't check it very carefully when I got it," she admitted. "I just tore open a corner to be sure it was the correct piece, then sent it out to have it framed. So I have no idea when a switch might have happened."

The little bells of the front door jangled, and we followed Julia back out to the gallery. A squat bald man stood at the entrance holding a framed picture—another piece of comic-book art.

"Julia, darling!" the man greeted.

"Hello, Ian," Julia said, giving him air kisses on each cheek. "I'm surprised to see you so soon! Are you looking for another panel?" She turned to Frank and me. "Ian Huntington, this is Frank and Joe Hardy. Ian is a big comic lover and just bought a page drawn by P. J. Rodriguez."

Now Ian looked sheepish. "Actually, Julia dear, I'm here to return the piece. Once I got it home, it just didn't work with my decor."

"Oh, I'm sorry to hear that." Julia looked disappointed, but she was gracious. "Would you like to see something else? I know you were interested in the Milners."

If I had the bucks, I'd be interested in the Milners too.

"Not today," said Ian. "I'm in a bit of a rush. But I will certainly be back! I think you are doing a great service, my dear. Thanks to you, comic-book art is finally getting the respect it deserves."

Julia smiled. "Thanks, Ian. It's great to have such a strong supporter."

Ian began spouting all kinds of arty theories about why comic-book art was so important. As my mind began wandering, my feet did too. I went and checked out the Milners.

I didn't care that comics were some kind of "new urban idiom" or about the "visual representation of a fragmented reality" that Ian was promoting. I thought the heroes were cool, the villains cooler, and the babes hot. Awesome action, great story lines—that's what I liked about them.

But it did get me wondering about the motives behind the forgery.

"So," I heard Frank say, "you think Julia's idea is going to take off?"

"Without a doubt," Ian said. "Julia is at the forefront of a lucrative new market just opening up. Always good to be ahead of the pack."

"If I'm too far ahead," said Julia ruefully, "I'll be out there all alone. Not everyone is as enthusiastic about it as you are. It's a big gamble."

"But a worthwhile one." Ian patted her cheek

in a fatherly way. "Now I have to dash. I need to register for the ComicCon."

"I'm sorry the Rodriguez didn't work out for you," Julia told him. "Would you like cash or a store credit?"

Ian shrugged. "Store credit is fine—as long as you keep repping the comic art."

"I'll do my very best!" Julia assured him.

Once Ian left, Julia took the framed P. J. Rodriguez drawing and leaned it against the wall. "I'll have to find a good place to hang it," she said. "P. J. comes in all the time. I hope he won't be disappointed about the return."

"Does that happen a lot?" Frank asked. "Returns?"

"Occasionally," Julia said. "Sometimes it's hard to know if the art will work for you until you get it home. Ian is pretty finicky. He once returned a poster because he thought it clashed with a rug."

The door chimes jangled again and a tall young guy wearing a worn leather jacket strode in. He flipped his sunglasses up to the top of his head, pushing his dark floppy curls away from his face. "Hi, Julia."

"P. J.!" Julia brightened. It was easy to see she liked him. "We were just talking about you."

"All good, I hope."

Julia introduced us and then pointed to the drawing leaning against the wall. "Sorry, but your lovely *Gremlin and Centaur* came back."

P. J. strode to the wall and picked up the picture. "This is a lovely gremlin and centaur," he said. "But it isn't mine."

He turned to face us. "This is a fake."

FRANK

4
Cartoon Criminal

"A fake?" Julia repeated, incredulous. "But—but that's not possible."

P. J. placed the drawing on the glass table in the corner. We all crowded around.

"See those really light lines?" P. J. pointed at the picture. "That's the sketch before it was inked. You'll find these ghost lines in most pictures— spots where the original hasn't been completely erased or covered by ink. But I always draw in blue. These ghosts are in black."

Julia's draw dropped. "I—can't believe it. Not another one!"

"What do you mean, *another* one? You have another forged picture of mine?" P. J. asked.

"Not yours," Julia said miserably. "Jeff Cohen's *Dark Hawk*."

"You're kidding!" P. J. exclaimed. "It's a fake? Man, that's rough."

Joe and I exchanged a look. P. J. must be an awfully close friend if she was telling him about the forgeries. Her whole reason for bringing us in rather than going to the police was so that as few people as possible would know about it.

P. J. must have been thinking the same thing. He raised an eyebrow and then glanced quickly at Joe and me.

"It's okay," Julia told him. "Frank and Joe are here to help get to the bottom of this."

"Oh, well, that's good."

I could tell he was a little dubious about us. He wouldn't be for long. I had a cool thought—once we solved the case, maybe he'd make us characters in one of his comics!

Julia rubbed her temples, as if this whole thing was giving her a wicked migraine. "Thank goodness Ian brought the drawing back. If he knew that I had sold him a forgery . . ."

"By accident," P. J. pointed out.

She shook her head. "It wouldn't matter. My reputation would be ruined. And he's one of my best

33

buyers—he's encouraged me all along about repping comic art." She sighed. "At least it's back at the gallery. I don't have to feel guilty that I cheated him!"

"By *accident*," P. J. repeated. "You didn't do anything wrong."

"But it's *my* responsibility," Julia argued. "Collectors trust the gallery to make sure everything is legit."

I could see this wasn't just business for Julia. This was a matter of honor. Doing the right thing. It made me like her even more—and the forger even less.

"Do you have any theories on how this happened?" I asked P. J.

P. J. scratched his head. "I suppose with *Dark Hawk*—well, that's been sold and resold so many times a forgery could have been introduced anywhere along the chain. But my own piece?" He shook his head. "I don't get it."

"The boards they're drawn on aren't very big," Joe pointed out. "It would be pretty easy to sneak one in or out of a storeroom."

"True," said Julia. "We have had a fair amount of traffic in and out of here getting ready for the comic-book convention."

I studied the drawing of the mythical creatures. "This one was in and out and back in again," I said.

Joe caught my meaning right away. "Ian could have bought it, swapped it for the fake, and then brought it back," he said.

SUSPECT PROFILE

Name: Ian Huntington

Hometown: San Francisco, California

Physical description: early fifties, 5' 7", 185 lbs., bald.

Occupation: Semi-retired

Background: Went to top business schools and worked in the financial world until he made a mint in several Internet investments. Works as a consultant to Internet start-up companies. Once he made his first million, he began to indulge in his passion for all things comics—began collecting in the last few years and has amassed a significant and valuable collection.

Suspicious behavior: Bought an original but returned a fake.

Suspected of: Forgery.

Possible motive: ?????? He has money, so that couldn't be it—so what could it be?

"Ian?" said Julia Her expression told me that he was not high on her suspect list. "I don't really see him doing something like that. He's a huge supporter of mine. And he isn't the only collector who returns art. It happens fairly frequently in this business." She scanned the walls and pointed at another P. J. Rodriquez. "Geoff Carter bought that one a few weeks ago and returned it yesterday."

P. J. sighed. "Is it something about my work?"

"Not at all," Julia quickly reassured him. "You'll find your buyers. I promise you."

"Still . . . ," I pressed.

Julia laughed. "I've seen Ian's sketches. He can't draw at all! There's no way he could pull off a forgery."

Despite my persistence, Julia seemed able to counter every one of my suspicions.

"The guy is famous for being loaded," P. J. added. "He can buy these—or sell them. Why get involved in forgeries that will only devalue his own collection?"

Okay. That clinched it. There didn't seem any way to come up with a motive for Ian. Time to move on.

"A lot of comics drawings are online," I reasoned. "Could a forger work from those?"

"Maybe . . . ," said Julia.

36

"That might explain how the forger made the mistake of the color of my sketches," P. J. said. "Even up close you have to look really hard to realize my ghost lines are blue."

"Why would someone forge comic-book art?" I asked. I always like to start with the motive. If you know why someone might commit a crime, it's a lot easier to try to figure out who.

"Same reason anyone would make a copy of any art," Julia said. "Greed."

"Or obsession," suggested P. J. "If someone was totally nuts about a piece of art, they could keep the original and sell the fake."

"Why anyone would be that obsessed over such childish material is beyond me," a voice said behind me.

I turned and saw a slim blond man, probably in his thirties, standing in the doorway. He had on a fashionable suit and tie.

He strode into the room. "Really, Julia," he said with a sneer. "This silly sideline of yours is going to make us a joke in the art world."

P. J. stiffened. Julia's eyes flicked to P. J., and her face tinged slightly pink. "Jasper, you know that's not true. We've already—"

Jasper cut her off. "I can't believe you actually think these babyish cartoons are art."

37

Whoa. This guy makes Simon on *Idol* seem like Paula.

"These kids will probably be your only customers," Jasper said, with a wave at Joe and me. "Not exactly a group with massive amounts of disposable income." He smirked at us. "Shouldn't you have outgrown comic books by now?"

This guy was really ticking me off.

"Graphic novels are now being reviewed in all the major papers," argued P.J. "There are graduate school courses in this art form, people write papers on their importance—"

"Oh please." Jasper rolled his eyes. "Talk to me when you can paint or draw like a true master, not just make silly sketches of superheroes and fairies." He strode away, went into his office, and slammed the door.

P. J. was so angry he was sputtering. He took a few steps toward Jasper's office.

"You wait and see!" he shouted at the closed door. "When I take my work to Monsters and Heroes you'll be sorry. Clyde Fanelli will be thrilled when I drop PopCulture for his gallery. He'll be laughing all the way to the bank."

He spun on his heels and headed for the door.

"P. J.! Please," Julia begged. "You know *I* don't feel that way! It's just Jasper—"

"That snob is going to be sorry," P. J. fumed. He raised his voice again so that Jasper would hear it through the door. "At least at Monsters and Heroes my work won't be stolen and copied."

Julia took a few stunned steps away from P. J. I guess she didn't think her friend would use her problems against her.

I couldn't totally blame the dude. He'd just found out his own work—an awesome drawing that must have taken forever to get perfect—had been stolen and copied. The gallery he trusted it to hadn't been able to prevent it. Then, on top of that, while he was being as gracious as possible about the theft, he gets totally dissed by Julia's partner. If it was me, I'd have popped Jasper one.

"P. J.," Julia said weakly.

P. J. just shook his head and stormed out the door.

Julia sank onto one of the little chairs at the table and covered her face with her hands. "This is awful," she moaned.

"You know, if this forgery just happened," Joe said, "it could happen again. The forger is still at it."

Julia's head snapped up. "Scotty Milner's drawings!" She raced to the two drawings of Frank "Fierce" Stone. She planted herself in front of them as if she were protecting them. "This forger has to be stopped before another piece of art is stolen and copied."

"And before word gets out," added Joe.

"Do you think P. J. will tell anyone?" I asked.

Julia let out a long slow sigh. "I don't know. In this mood . . ." Her voice trailed off.

"Who's Clyde Fanelli?" I asked. "P. J. mentioned him."

Julia made a face. "He owns Monsters and Heroes. As soon as he heard that I was trying this new thing—representing comic-book art—he claimed he had the idea ages ago."

"Is that possible?" Joe wondered.

Julia snorted. "Anything's possible. But he certainly never mentioned it before—or approached any artists to represent."

"Sounds like he's just jumping on your bandwagon," I said.

"And he's trying to grab the artists who have already agreed to go with me. I don't have very many—I think artists are waiting to see how it works out."

"So you're the first gallery doing this?" I asked. "I'm surprised. It does seem like a great idea."

Julia nodded. "Usually the artists sell their originals directly, often at the conventions. It's why

Jasper is so down on it. If this venture fails, the gallery will look really bad—you know, following the wrong trend."

"It will look even worse if it's known for selling forgeries," I pointed out.

I wish I hadn't. Julia looked as if I'd kicked her in the stomach.

Joe checked his watch. "We need to go. Chet's waiting."

"Okay." I turned to Julia. "I think our investigation will really begin at the convention. We'll learn a lot there. In the meantime, if you could write up a list of anyone you think might benefit from selling the forgeries, that would be great."

"Thanks so much for doing this," said Julia.

"See you tomorrow morning," Joe said, and then we left.

"P. J. went pretty ballistic," I noted as we hurried to Union Square. "I hope he doesn't go to that other gallery. Julia really needs him."

"Yeah," Joe said thoughtfully. "And that would make Clyde Fanelli very happy. I wonder if Clyde would stoop to something like this to undermine Julia's new business. He'd know that P. J. would immediately see that the piece was a forgery."

"Only because Ian brought it back," I pointed out. "It's a good thing it didn't match his sofa or whatever. Otherwise we wouldn't know that the *Dark Hawk* forgery isn't an isolated incident."

"And we wouldn't have been alerted that the forger is still at it," said Joe.

"It does sound like Julia is onto something big with this new sideline."

"Jasper doesn't think so," Joe noted. "In fact, he'd be thrilled if these forgeries tanked her business before it could really get started."

"But wouldn't that ruin him, too?" I asked.

"Not if he put all the blame on Julia," Joe reasoned. "It's really obvious that he has no interest in the comic art, so no one would think the art he handles is fake."

"So we have two suspects to start with," I said. "The rival owner and Julia's partner."

"And then there are all the other suspects we haven't thought of yet."

Chet was sitting on a bench in Union Square. He was surrounded by shopping bags and guide books, and he was studying a brochure.

"Hey, Chet!" I called. We jogged over. He was beaming.

"I got you your registration kits," he said, handing us each a plastic bag with SF COMICCON blazed across it. I pulled open the drawstring and saw schedules, little goodies like keychains and

42

pencils, and even a mini comic book.

"This is going to be so awesome," Chet declared. "All my favorite artists are here! I signed up for the P. J. Rodriguez and Eloise Winston signings. Scotty Milner tickets were already snapped up."

I scanned the program. The organizers promised raffles, panel discussions, signings, movies, and many, many surprises.

I hoped one of the surprises would be how quickly we solved the case.

5.

Wild Ride

The whole jet lag, time difference, and nearly being offed by a clown had finally taken its toll. I was beat. Judging by how deflated Chet and Frank looked, I wasn't the only one.

"How about we grab a bite back near the hotel and then turn in?" I said as we walked to the cable car stop.

Frank grabbed my arm and pressed his palm against my forehead.

"What are you doing?" I asked, swatting away his hand.

"Checking to see if you have a fever," he teased. "I think this is the first time I ever heard you suggesting an early bedtime!"

"Ha, ha." My brother, the jokester.

We climbed aboard the crowded cable car. The conductor rang the bell, the middle guy pushed on the lever, and we lurched uphill. Cable cars took a lot of effort to run.

"Most of these kids were registering at the convention today," Chet observed.

I glanced around. You didn't have to be an expert detective to figure out that a lot of these passengers were into comics. I spotted four T-shirts advertising the upcoming comic-based move *Millennium*, two T-shirts with comic strips on the back, and comic-book characters staring out at me from five others.

The big clue? All those plastic bags with SF COMICCON printed on them.

"No way," a guy behind me said. "Scotty Milner is totally tired. P. J. has it all over him."

"Are you crazy or are you stupid?" another kid responded. "If you think P. J. tops Scotty, you're one or the other."

"I heard that Scotty just wants to make movies now," said a girl.

"No way!" someone gasped. "What about the books?"

"His movies aren't anywhere near as good as his books. Why does he let them make them so bad?"

I kept listening, hoping to overhear something

that could be useful for the case. Mostly I learned that gossip ruled the comic-book world.

One good thing: No one was talking about the forgery. With the way rumors spread in this scene, that meant no one had heard about it.

Yet.

The cable car chugged its way up and down the famous San Francisco hills. There were times when I seriously thought we were pointing straight up or straight down. I was surprised we didn't have seat belts. If these things moved faster, a cable ride would be as wild a ride as a roller coaster.

"No way is Glintz going to turn out to be bad," Chet said beside me. He had joined one of the debates. "That would be too obvious."

"But that's the beauty," a girl argued. "It's so obvious, no one will suspect it!"

Glintz was a demon type in a comic I didn't really follow. But clearly most of the people on this cable car had an opinion.

We lurched to a stop in Chinatown. To make room for a lady with a little kid, Frank and I stood and clung to the poles on the outside of the cable car. I just hoped we didn't pass anything with side mirrors. I'd get clipped!

I could hear two girls arguing in the middle of the car. So far everyone had expressed pretty strong opinions but kept it under control. These girls were actually shouting.

"You don't know what you're talking about, loser!"

People tried to give the two girls room. I spotted the adversaries: two college-age girls dressed in goth gear. The one with the blue streaks in her jet-black hair was Asian American. The one with the short, spiky magenta hair was smaller, with super-pale skin.

Suddenly Magenta shoved Blue Streaks. "You know I'm right!" she shrieked. "Admit it."

"I won't admit anything," Blue Streaks screamed back. "You're just jealous!"

A crowded cable car with open sides was not the best place for a shoving match.

"Settle down, girls!" one of the conductors shouted. But the car was so crowded, I didn't think he could actually see what was happening.

"Don't make us stop this car!" the other conductor shouted. But he had to keep his hand on the brakes and his eye on traffic.

"Take that back!" Now Magenta shoved the taller Blue Streaks really hard. Blue Streaks stumbled, and her notebook went flying between Frank and me.

"My drawings!" Blue Streaks wailed.

In a flash, she climbed over the seat. Just as she was about to jump off, I grabbed her around the waist and held her back.

And watched Frank hurl himself off the cable car and into the street.

6.

Keeping Secrets

The minute I landed (okay, stumbled) onto the pavement I knew I had done something really dumb. Jump off a moving cable car? Sheesh! That's something Joe would do. But I saw that notebook go flying, and something kicked in and I had to get it.

Luckily for me, cable cars don't go so fast, so all I did was lose my balance on the steep hill. I scrambled back up, grabbed the notebook, and chased after the cable car. I didn't want to get separated from Chet and Joe. My map was in the ComicCon goodie bag, and I had no idea where I was right now.

I darted through pedestrians up the hill and

made it to the cable car stop before it took off again. I leaped aboard.

"Are you nuts?" the back conductor scolded me. "I should put you off for pulling a stunt like that."

"Sorry," I said. "I just wanted to get the notebook back."

"A hero type. This is your only warning. And if your girlfriend gets into another fight, she's off too."

"She's not my girlfriend—"

The bell clanged and cut me off. I slowly made my way forward through the car.

"I can't believe you did that!" Blue Streaks gushed when I handed her the notebook. She flung her arms around my neck.

"Uh, well, you're welcome."

The girl who did the shoving looked slightly ashamed. But only slightly. "I hope you're okay," she said to me.

Not exactly an apology, but whatever. She moved away to a different part of the car.

Blue Streaks let me go and lovingly stroked her notebook. "I can't believe you threw yourself off the cable car to save my pictures."

Now that I took a closer look, I realized it wasn't a notebook, but an artist's sketch pad.

She looked up at me. "Oh, I'm sorry. I'm Becky Chang."

"Frank Hardy," I told her. "And my brother Joe is the guy who kept you from flying off the cable car."

"Thank you, too," Becky said to Joe. "I guess that would have been kinda dumb for me to do."

"But you're glad my brother was dumb enough to do it for you," teased Joe.

Becky giggled. "I guess you're right about that. But you have to understand—I'm going to meet with Scotty Milner and show him my drawings. It's the opportunity of a lifetime!"

"You got a ticket?" Chet asked. "You are so lucky."

Now Becky looked at Chet. "Are you going to the con too?"

"We all are," said Joe.

"Did you know that Milner got the idea for the character of Rigsby the Rat from his junior high school principal?" Chet asked.

"Really?" Becky's eyes lit up. "I use people from school in my drawings all the time." She bit a lethal-looking nail. "I'm kind of nervous about meeting Scotty. He's so intimidating! And my stuff is more like the comics P. J. Rodriguez draws.

51

I'm hoping I can find a way to talk to him."

"P. J. Rodriguez?" Joe piped up. "I think we—"

"Ooh, this is my stop!" Becky popped up. "I have to grab a bus the rest of the way. I live in Haight-Ashbury."

"See you at the con," Chet said.

Becky climbed down from the cable car. I noticed Magenta got off at the same stop. I wondered if that was going to be bad. They exchanged some snarls and then Magenta disappeared into a coffee shop.

We made it the rest of the way to Fisherman's Wharf without anyone or anything flying off the cable car. But it did get me thinking that maybe something without open sides would be a safer way to get around.

"Wow, this place is packed," said Chet as we strolled along Pier 39. The pier was an awesome place—it had a theater, an aquarium, a carousel, shops, and lots of little places to eat on two different levels. We grabbed a table at an outdoor café overlooking the water and ordered.

After the waitress left, Chet pulled out the convention program.

"Is there a map of the booths?" Joe asked.

Chet handed him a sheet of paper. Joe spread it out on the table.

"There's a lot going on," he commented.

"Check this out," I said, poking at the map. "This whole line of booths is set up just to sell comic-book art."

Joe nodded. "I wonder if anyone there has heard about forgeries. We should—"

I gave him a quick kick.

"Ow!" he yelped. "What—" Then he caught my glare.

"Sorry," I said with a smile. "I thought that was the table leg."

"No prob," Joe grumbled.

Chet stared at us, puzzled. "Why would anyone be talking about forgeries?" Then his eyes narrowed. "Are you guys—?"

Chet believed that we sometimes did amateur detective work. He had no idea we were with ATAC. And it had to stay that way.

"Hey, look," I said quickly. "Here come our sandwiches. Man, those fries look good!"

We had to be more careful. The hardest part of the case might be hiding it from our best friend.

7.

"F" Is for Fans

Okay, I admit it. I'm into comics. I love the classics—
Batman, *Sandman*—but I also love the newer stuff.
Scotty Milner's *Fierce*, P. J. Rodriguez, *Demon Seed-
lings*. All of them. And Chet—he's a total comics
nut. He could definitely win a comic trivia game
show. But we were amateurs compared to the
crowd the first morning of the convention.

Now I knew why the word "fan" is short for
"fanatic."

"Whoa, buddy," I said to a guy dressed as Batman. "I can only move so fast."

He wasn't the only Batman. I counted six of
them just as we tried to make it through the door.
I also spotted four Glitzels, six Dooms, and three
Shizzlers. There were also costumes of characters

I'd never seen before. Or maybe that was just standard comic-geek attire.

Other than the costumed hard-core fans, the crowd was really varied—guys, girls, all ages, all types. You name it, they were all here.

And there might even be a forger among them.

We showed our registration badges at the entrance and were shoved by the crowd into a gigantic room. Booths created a maze of aisles. There was a small stage at one end of the main floor, and all around were gigantic TV monitors screening clips.

The noise was deafening—between the movie clips, the interviews blasting from videos at the booths, and the enormous crowd, I could barely hear Chet. He nudged me again.

"Scotty Milner straight ahead," he said.

I glanced toward a bunch of flashing lights. Photographers three deep were snapping pictures of a guy in his twenties with short, cropped blond hair. His tight black T-shirt revealed major muscles. Clearly he knew his way around a gym. He cruised through the swarm like a rock star.

"Scotty! This way!" shouted a photographer.

Without breaking stride, Scotty flashed the guy a—well, not a smile, exactly. It was more like a tough-guy sneer *pretending* to be a smile.

"Scotty! Scotty! Sign my book!" Several girls held out comic books to their hero. Some guys, too.

"So that's Scotty Milner," Frank said. "I thought he'd be older."

"Nah, he started in the business as a teenager," Chet informed us. "He was one of the youngest artists ever to create a bidding war between publishers."

"Who's that dude?" I pointed out a scowling man in his twenties with a bunch of piercings.

"Jeff Cahey," Chet told us. "Another artist."

"Looks like he hates Scotty Milner," said Frank.

"They were at school together. Everyone thought Jeff would be the one with all the success."

"Sure didn't turn out that way," I said, watching Milner and his entourage part the crowds. This was beyond rock star—the way people were behaving made Scotty Milner seem like royalty!

"I have to get to the auditorium," said Chet, checking his schedule. "There's a panel discussion on trends in heroes and villains."

"I want to check out the booths," Frank said.

"Yeah, and maybe get a Scotty Milner autograph," I added.

"That would be worth money," Chet said.

True. As long as it wasn't a fake!

As soon as Chet took off for his panel discussion,

Frank and I studied the convention map.

"Okay, Julia's gallery has a booth set up down that way," Frank said. "Retail Row."

We were in Scotty Milner's wake, so it was tough going. Around us were booths set up by stores selling comics and related items. Farther along, I remembered, were the publishers' booths, which was probably where Milner was headed.

"Hi, Julia," I heard Scotty Milner say up ahead. He must be stopping by her booth. Frank and I squeezed through the crowd so we could be there too.

"Hey, P. J.'s with her," Frank whispered.

"I guess he stopped being mad," I said. "That's good."

"Scotty!" said Julia. "Hi! Look—I've got your drawings on display."

"Hey, Milner," P. J. said. He didn't look overly excited.

Scotty nodded. "'Sup, P. J.?"

P. J. shrugged. "Not selling my soul to Hollywood."

Scotty's jaw set. "You should be so lucky—or talented."

Whoa. No love lost there.

"So, Scotty," Julia said, obviously trying to keep the peace, "are you here all three days?"

"I suppose," Scotty said. "My public demands it."

P. J. rolled his eyes. I couldn't blame him. Scotty did seem sort of full of himself. I hoped that Chet wouldn't be crushed if he found out that Milner was kind of a jerk. But then I realized—Chet probably already knew that. He knows all things comics.

"You are really doing artists a service," Scotty told Julia. "I'm so glad I'm not trying to sell my own work. This way I can concentrate on the art—not the commerce. Lesser artists"—he glanced toward P. J.—"can gain a great deal if you were to take an interest."

"So you think this is a good trend?" asked Frank.

Scotty's head whipped around. He must be one of those guys who forget that other people can speak while he was pontificating. "How's that?"

"Putting the comic-book art into galleries and selling it that way," Frank persisted. I knew he wanted to get a bead on how the artists felt about Julia's venture.

"Absolutely. Why?" Scotty demanded, his blue eyes narrowing. "Don't you think we're true artists?"

Frank look startled by the abrupt switch in Scotty's tone. "Totally," Frank assured him. "I had my eye on that *Fierce* sketch," he added, pointing toward the drawing of Milner's famous detective.

That seemed to placate Scotty. "Ah, well, good. Even P. J. here should get the respect he deserves as an artist. Isn't that right, Rodriguez?"

P. J. ignored Scotty. Instead he held up one of Julia's catalogs and pretended to read it.

"So you're allowing PopCulture to be your representative?" a woman standing nearby asked. I noticed she had a small reporter's notebook and was with one of the photographers.

Scotty glanced around. Who was he looking for? Then I realized he was looking toward the Monsters and Heroes booth, just a few feet down. "I think Julia is a wonderful gallery owner," he said, hedging his bets. "And she has two of my own personal favorites."

"Ah, yes," the woman said with a smile. "Frank 'Fierce' Stone."

"See you, Julia." Scotty turned and began to make his way down the row. A large crowd followed him. Once he had left the booth, there was no one there. Everyone had been at Julia's booth because of Scotty.

"Scotty Milner has a lot of power in this scene," I commented to Frank. I said it quietly so that P. J.

wouldn't hear. He'd already had his ego bashed by Milner.

Frank nodded. "If he allows Julia to be his exclusive rep, that could put her gallery on the map."

"Make her loads of money, too," I added.

"Only it's not going to happen if Scotty finds out that she's now had two forgeries," said Frank.

I watched Milner's progress down the row of booths. He nodded at the burly, tattooed man who stood at the Monsters and Heroes booth. That must be Clyde Fanelli. He didn't look like the art world type. He looked like he belonged on a pirate ship, not selling collectible pirates.

Scotty didn't stop, so the crowd didn't either. This seemed like a good time to check out the competition.

"Come on." I strode down the row toward the Monsters and Heroes booth.

"What can I show you boys?" Clyde Fanelli asked.

I glanced around his booth. He carried some of the same type of items Julia did: paintings based on famous characters, figurines and other collectibles, books on—you guessed it—monsters and heroes.

"Do you have anything like that other booth?" Frank asked, jerking his thumb toward Julia's

PopCulture booth. "The comic-book art?"

Fanelli's eyes narrowed. "Not yet. But I will soon."

That got my attention. So he really was hoping to steal the artists away from Julia.

"And I'd stay away from that gallery," Fanelli added. Gleefully, I thought. "I've heard they sell fakes."

Whoa. This was not good news for Julia. Word was out.

"Oh, yeah?" I said. "Maybe you just want to diss that gallery because it's your competition."

"I don't play those games, kids," Fanelli replied. "Don't need to."

Like I believed that. There were more people stopping by Julia's booth than Fanelli's—thanks to the Scotty Milner drawings and P. J. Rodriguez hanging out there.

"That's just gossip," said Frank. "I've heard lots of rumors today, and the doors just opened an hour ago!"

"The forgeries are no rumor," Fanelli insisted. "I know this for a fact."

We knew it for a fact too. What I wanted to know was how *he* found out.

"Where'd you hear this so-called fact?" I asked,

"Direct from the horse's mouth," declared Fanelli.

"I got the inside scoop from Jasper Scranton, the co-owner of PopCulture."

I had to work hard not to let my jaw drop. Julia's partner was leaking the news about the forgeries? He had to know how bad this was for business.

"And," Fanelli continued, rubbing his beefy hands together, "I can't wait to tell Scotty Milner all about it. Don't think he'd want that little lady to rep him with that kind of reputation."

I didn't think he would either.

But was Jasper just a big blabbermouth? Or was he behind the forgeries to sink Julia's comic-book art prospects?

8.
A Clue!

What was Jasper Scranton thinking? Why would he tell his biggest competition about the forgery? Was he stupid?

Or was he up to something?

That's what Joe and I had to find out. We left Clyde Fanelli and studied the convention map again.

"There's a room for artists selling their own stuff," Joe said.

"The way it's usually done," I added.

"Let's find out if any of them have heard the rumor—and if Clyde has been talking to them about coming to his gallery."

We left Retail Row and found the Artists' Area. Here the artists themselves had work displayed for sale.

<u>SUSPECT PROFILE</u>

<u>Name:</u> Jasper Scranton

<u>Hometown:</u> Originally from New York City, moved to San Francisco after college

<u>Physical description:</u> Age 31, 5' 11", 195 lbs., blond, wavy hair cut short, well-dressed.

<u>Occupation:</u> Half-owner of PopCulture Gallery

<u>Background:</u> Art history major at an Ivy League school, took art classes himself but realized he'd never make it as an artist. Previously worked as an assistant at an art auction house.

<u>Suspicious behavior:</u> Spreading the very bad news of the forgery at the convention.

<u>Suspected of:</u> Forgery.

<u>Possible motive:</u> Hates comic-book art—might want to ruin Julia's new venture.

"Hey," said Joe. "It's that girl who shoved Becky on the cable car."

Sure enough, the petite girl with the spiky

magenta hair was standing in front of a large movie poster for a film based on a comic-book series called *Freakster*.

She must have felt us looking at her. She glanced our way and frowned. She seemed to have trouble placing us.

"Hi there," Joe said, strolling up to her. Of course. He sees a pretty girl—even an extreme goth girl who got into a fight on public transportation— and he has to go introduce himself. Shaking my head, I followed him over.

"How do I know you?" she asked.

"You got into it on a cable car with Becky Chang," Joe told her.

She looked slightly embarrassed. "Oh, yeah." She looked up at me. "And you're that guy who went all Han Solo for her."

Now I was the one turning pink. "That's not exactly—"

"Whatever." The girl shrugged. "If you like cheaters, that's your own problem."

"Is that what your fight was about?" Joe asked. "Cheating?"

Now the girl looked angry, as if just thinking about it made her mad all over again. "Becky Chang pretends to be all sweet and nice. But look out. She's not the angel she makes herself out to be."

To be honest, the goth getup had already told me that.

"Look I don't know you—so I don't want to get all up in your business," the girl said.

"I'm Frank and this is my brother, Joe," I said. "There. Now you know us. What's your name?"

Now the girl smiled. "Mandy Kittson. Okay. I now know you well enough to butt in. Look, if you're into comics, then Becky will be into you. But be careful. She is super ambitious. She doesn't care who she hurts to get ahead. And she wants to make it in comics really bad."

"It looked to me like you were the one picking on her," Joe pointed out. "You were doing the shoving."

"Because she stole an idea from me," Mandy snapped. "She took my concept and even some of my work for my senior project. Now I have to start all over again."

"What do you mean?" I asked. An idea was forming, and I needed more info.

"Becky and I are both seniors at the San Francisco Art School. My sketch pad went missing. Becky found it. Was it just a coincidence that she didn't return until *after* she handed in her proposal? And that it was almost identical to what was in my pad?"

"Can you prove that?" asked Joe.

Mandy shook her head. "It's just too hard to prove which came first. And because she handed hers in before me, it was already approved. She draws faster than anyone else at school. She's kind of a phenom."

"If only she'd use her powers for good, not evil, am I right?" Joe said.

"I had to come up with a completely different idea, all because she stole mine. It's just not fair."

No, it wasn't. If what Mandy was saying was true—a big if—it could mean that Becky might be one of our suspects. That sketch pad I rescued for her was filled with her comics drawings. She had clearly hoped to have a career in graphic novels.

Art school probably cost a lot of money. That could be a motive. And she worked fast—making it possible for her to have committed the forgeries quickly and make the little mistakes, too.

"Listen, I'm supposed to meet my boyfriend at the screening room," said Mandy. "Are you going?"

I spotted Becky coming into the arts exhibition area. "No, I think we'll check out the art."

"Okay. Well, I'll probably see you around."

"I didn't think goth was your type," I told Joe as

he watched Mandy walk away. "Besides, she has a boyfriend."

Joe shrugged. "No harm in looking, right?"

"Well, right now let's go take a look at what Becky is studying so intently." She hadn't moved from her spot since I first saw her.

We came up beside Becky. She was staring at a drawing so hard she never noticed us.

"Hi, Becky," I said.

She started, then smiled. "My hero! My two heroes," she greeted us, giving us each a quick hug.

"So, you like this one?" I asked. We were standing in front of a small drawing. It was an old classic—back before digital. You could see that it was colored by hand.

Becky nodded. "I love the old style. But you have to see them in person."

"Why's that?" Joe asked.

"To see the strokes. And sometimes the colors aren't quite the same when they're reproduced. That's why it's important to see them up close."

Important to make sure a forgery is accurate? I wondered—if she would copy a classmate's work, would she also copy a famous comic-book artist?

We needed to get her talking. I looked to my brother for help, but he had stepped back a ways and was holding up his camera.

"Smile, bro!" he called.

A burly security guard clamped a beefy hand on Joe's shoulder. "No pictures," the guard snarled.

Joe looked up into the guy's big face. "Sorry. I didn't know."

The guard pointed at a sign. Okay. It was kind of hard to miss. But we had other things on our minds.

"Read that," the guard instructed.

"'Absolutely no photos allowed,'" Joe mumbled. "Sorry."

"If I see you do it again, I'll confiscate your camera."

"No need," said Joe. "See? I'm putting it away right now."

Satisfied, the guard returned to his post and Joe rejoined us.

"Well, that was embarrassing," he said.

"Yeah. It's a dumb rule," Becky agreed.

"I don't know," I said. "Taking photos is one way to make forgeries, or unlicensed products like T-shirts. That's ripping off the artists who work really hard."

I watched Becky for her reaction.

"I should get going," she said. "There's so much more to see!" She spun around and left the exhibition area.

Hmm. Did I make her uncomfortable by mentioning forgeries—and reminding her that she's ripping off artists? Or did she really just want to check out the other booths?

"Well, there goes that idea," Joe grumbled.

"What idea?" I asked.

"I wanted to take a picture of one of the covers and Photoshop Chet into it," Joe explained. "That would be the coolest birthday card."

"It would," I agreed. "But it ain't gonna happen."

"So where to now?" asked Joe.

I was stuck. I wasn't really sure what to do to get to the bottom of this forgery mess.

As I mulled over our next move, I noticed a bulked-up tattooed guy standing by the movie poster, holding a very distinctive cell phone. The thing was metallic blue with silver lightning bolts on the back.

Only he wasn't using it to talk. He was using it to snap a picture.

I grabbed Joe's arm.

"Yow," he yelped. "What's with you?"

"That guy," I hissed, nodding toward the dude with the wicked cool cell. "He's taking pictures."

"No fair! I get nailed and he gets away with it. Where's that security guard now?"

"Too late," I said. The guy was gone. It was

going to be hard trailing people at this convention. There were just too many fans!

"That might be a way to make the forgeries," Joe pointed out, still scanning the crowd for the guy.

"Maybe," I said. "But Julia thinks she had the originals at some point. That means someone took them, made the forgeries, and gave her back the fakes."

"It's still something to think about. The forger could have started from a photo and put in the final touches once he—"

"Or she," I put in.

"Or *she* had possession of the drawing. That way it wouldn't have to have been out of Julia's sight for very long."

We went back to Julia's booth. P. J. wasn't there anymore, but Ian Huntington, the man who had returned P. J.'s picture, was.

"Why isn't the *Dark Hawk* picture on display?" Ian was asking Julia. "Don't you want everyone to see it? Generate publicity for the auction."

Sticky. Julia couldn't tell her biggest buyer that the piece wasn't hanging because it was a fake. How was she going to get out of this?

"Oh, the *Dark Hawk*, well, uh, yes," Julia stammered.

I wanted to help her out, but my brain was fresh out of excuses.

"The frame," she blurted. "I wasn't happy with it, so I sent it back out."

That answer seemed to satisfy Ian. "Yes, a beauty like the *Dark Hawk* needs the proper setting," he said. "Well, I look forward to the auction." He wandered off.

"That was good thinking," I said.

Julia's forehead crinkled. "Frames," she murmured.

"What is it?" Joe asked.

"The P. J. Rodriguez drawing that Ian returned. It was in a new frame."

I knew where she was heading. "The switch could have happened at the framer's."

Finally! An actual clue to investigate! I was getting kind of antsy just hanging around the con. I mean, it was cool to be there, but I couldn't really enjoy it, since I was supposed to be keeping my eyes and ears open for the forger.

"Let's find Ian and ask him where he had the Rodriguez reframed," I suggested, searching for Ian's bald head in the crowd.

"Let's not," said Julia firmly. "I don't want to draw attention to the problem until we get to the bottom of this. Framers often put their own labels on the back, so it should be easy to check."

"So let's hit the gallery," I urged. "Look for the labels."

"I can't get away," Julia said, glancing around her booth. "And Jasper said he'd be out all day at an estate sale. Can you check for me?"

"Of course!" said Joe. I could tell he was also glad to have something concrete to pursue. If the two forgeries were framed at the same place, we finally had a solid lead.

Julia fumbled in her purse, searching for her keys. She pulled out a set and held it out to me. "The square-shaped one—"

A bloodcurdling shriek cut off the rest of her sentence.

9.
Superhero Action!

I hear a girl scream in terror and I don't wait to ask questions.

I pushed through the crowd. The girl screamed again.

There she was—a gorgeous red-haired girl struggling with a beefy thug with a ski mask over his face. He had her from behind, his thick arms wrapped around her waist. Her knees buckled, and he started to drag her toward the stairs.

I couldn't believe it! People just stood there—watching! Taking pictures, even!

"Yah!" I shouted, flinging myself onto the surprised thug. I knocked the girl and her attacker to the floor. The thug was so shocked he released her. She rolled out of the way.

The thug managed to flip me off him. He was on his feet in a flash.

"Are you nuts?" he shouted at me.

Did he think he was so hard-core that only a crazy person would try to stop him? *He* was the crazy one! Only a madman would attack a girl in a crowded convention center.

I didn't waste breath with an answer. The dude was a lot bigger than me, so I needed an advantage. I hurled myself at his knees. He toppled, landing with a thud. I scrambled on top of him.

Oof! I went sprawling onto the ground. An accomplice sideswiped me! And sat on top of me.

I craned my neck to see my attacker.

The red-haired girl!

"You're ruining everything," she hissed at me.

Next thing I knew there was fog and loud music. A strange figure descended on a rope from the ceiling, landing just a few feet away.

Uh-oh. Truth was dawning.

I recognized the silver bodysuit and winged boots. *Mercury*. A comic-book superhero about to star in his own movie.

"I thought *I* was supposed to rescue the girl," the actor dressed as Mercury said. He was obviously having a hard time keeping a straight face. "Looks like I have to rescue the bad guy instead."

The crowd laughed as Mercury helped up the thug, who pulled off his ski cap and rubbed the back of his head. I hoped the guy had a sense of humor. I'd knocked him hard.

The red-haired girl stood up and smoothed her pink skirt. I pushed myself off the floor and got vertical more slowly. I didn't really want to face the actors—or the laughing audience.

"You're supposed to be Maggie Murphy, aren't you?" I asked the girl.

"Yup. Red hair and everything. And you barged into a reenactment of a scene in the movie—a scene you're not in."

"Sorry." My face was redder than the girl's hair. I tried to slip away, but Mercury slung his arm over my shoulder.

"Let's hear it for our surprise guest!" he announced. "It's nice to know that chivalry isn't dead."

The crowd laughed and clapped, so I gave them a sheepish wave. Mercury's fingers dug into my shoulder. I guess he was more ticked off than he was letting on. And he wasn't even the guy I hit!

Frank stepped out of the crowd. "Man," he hooted, "I wish Chet was here to see that performance."

"I wish *no one* saw that performance," I grumbled.

"That makes two of us," a blond woman said. She held a clipboard and looked seriously peeved. "You ruined the first scene!"

"Hey, I didn't know! I thought the girl was being attacked!" Sheesh. Why doesn't anyone give me props for risking my neck for a stranger?

Mercury grinned. It was kind of weird to be talking to a guy covered in silver makeup. "What do you think, Rachel? Should we add our good Samaritan to the act?"

"Remind him that the fights aren't real, okay?" the thug said, joining us.

"Hey, man," I said. "I'm really sorry."

"My brother has a bad habit of acting before thinking," said Frank.

Way to stand up for me, bro.

"That's okay. It was an honest mistake," the thug-actor said.

"This isn't funny," said Rachel. "The movie people paid a lot of money for you actors to perform scenes that will get people excited about an action film. It's not a comedy."

"Believe me, it won't happen again," I promised.

"Make sure that it doesn't," Rachel snapped.

"Not until you take some acting classes," Mercury joked.

"Thanks for trying to save me," the girl said.

Finally, some appreciation!

"Enough chit-chat," Rachel declared. "We have to set up the next scene upstairs near the auditorium. And you"—she poked my chest with her clipboard—"I don't want to see you anywhere nearby!"

"Not a problem."

Rachel rounded up her performers and led them away.

"So . . . ," Frank began.

"Don't even," I cut him off. I had taken enough ribbing already.

"There you are!" a voice called.

"P. J.!" shouted a fan in the crowd.

Sure enough, a distraught P. J. Rodriguez loped toward us.

"Look, it's P. J.!" someone else cried.

P. J. ignored the fans and grabbed my arm. He pulled me close to Frank. "We have to find a place to talk," he said in a low voice.

I nodded. "Sure thing."

"This way," Frank said. He led us to a stairwell I hadn't even noticed. Frank is into details like that. It makes us a good team.

Once inside the stairwell P. J. leaned against the wall, shaking his head. I could tell something serious was up.

"What is it?" I asked. "Did something happen to Julia?"

"No, it's this." He pulled a large envelope out of his leather jacket.

I opened it and took out a drawing.

Frank peered over my shoulder. "What is it?" he asked.

I recognized P. J.'s style, but I didn't know the picture.

"It's a preliminary sketch for some new characters I'm working on," P. J. told us. "Someone dropped it off at Julia's booth addressed to me."

"How did the person get your page?" I asked.

"It's not my page," P. J. said. "It's another fake."

My jaw dropped.

"Why would the forger do this?" asked Frank. "Send a forgery to the artist himself?"

"I have no idea," P. J. said, exasperated.

I felt for the guy. It must be a drag to think that your incredibly original work could be copied so well. It was sort of an insult.

"Extortion, maybe?" Frank suggested. "Maybe he'll flood the market with fakes unless you pay him off?"

"Could be . . ." I had another thought. "Maybe the forger is just bragging. There seems to be a fair amount of ego running around this convention."

"Whatever the reason," P. J. said, "I want it stopped."

"Standard envelope," noted Frank. "No return address. No postmark."

"So it's someone who's registered for the convention," I said. "Did Julia see anyone drop it off?"

P. J. shook his head. "She was swamped."

"You said these are new ideas," Frank said. "So they've never been published."

"Right," said P.J.

"How could they copy something from your sketchbook?" I asked.

"I posted some pages on my blog," P. J. said. "Anyone could have seen it."

That didn't narrow down the suspect list much.

I studied the fake. "I thought comics were done in just a few standard sizes. This is a lot smaller."

"There's an art supply store here that makes specialty sketchbooks," P. J. explained. "That's what I use when I'm first coming up with ideas."

"Can we keep this?" I asked.

"Please. I don't ever want to see it again."

"We'll look into this," Frank promised. "Maybe someone at the art supply store can tell us who bought paper just like yours."

"Thanks. I've got to get to a panel discussion on magic in comics," said P. J. "But keep me posted the minute you find out anything." He dashed up the stairs, two at a time.

"We've got to get over to PopCulture," Frank reminded me. "We have frames to check out."

We hurried to the gallery. I really hoped this would turn into a solid lead.

We were right across the street from PopCulture when Frank put his hand on my arm. "Hang on," he said.

"What's up?"

"Julia gave us the keys because Jasper wasn't going to be at the gallery all day, right?"

"Yeah, so?"

"So why is the door wide open?"

10.

Break-in—or Break in the Case?

I went into stealth mode. This could be a burglary in progress—we had to be careful.

I nodded at Joe. Keeping close to the wall and with my eyes peeled, I snuck into the gallery with Joe right behind me. The main room was empty. My guess was that whoever was in the gallery was checking out the storeroom.

With my back against the wall, I listened hard enough to make my ears hurt. Nothing.

I raised my eyebrows at Joe. He tipped his head toward the hallway.

I slowly moved my head to peek around the corner. Empty.

My heart thudded. It only just occurred to me that we probably should have called the cops before investigating a possible burglary in progress. Too late now. If I tried making a call now, the burglar would hear me and book it out the back door.

I hoped the burglar wasn't armed.

We slid down the hall, making as little noise as possible. That's when I heard it: a voice, coming from Jasper Scranton's office.

Joe and I stood on either side of Jasper's closed office door. I could hear Jasper talking to someone.

"Hey, wasn't he—," Joe started.

I made a sharp move and held a finger to my lips. I hoped my expression told him how dumb it was to talk right now.

He got the message. He pressed his ear against the door. I did the same.

"I'm sure she'll see the light now," Jasper said. "With all the problems that stupid comic art is causing? She's got to drop the whole thing. Then we can concentrate on the kind of art we should be carrying."

Interesting. He actually sounded pleased about the trouble Julia was in. This put him at the top of the suspect list. He had the opportunity, and I just heard a motive. With his art world contacts, he could also probably find himself a forger. It was adding up.

"I don't think she can risk it anymore. Not with this latest incident."

Could he be talking about the picture P. J. had just shown us?

I heard him laugh, which really annoyed me. How could he be enjoying Julia's predicament? They might be partners, but they certainly weren't friends. I wondered how they knew each other.

Suddenly the door opened. Joe and I stumbled right into Jasper, who was still holding his phone. "Hey!" he yelped, looking startled.

I caught Joe's elbow and we straightened back up.

"Got a couple of eavesdroppers," Jasper said into the phone. "I'll call you back." He clicked off and glared at us.

"Well?" he said.

"We didn't think you'd be here," Joe said.

"Yeah, we were worried the gallery was being burglarized," I added. It's always good to stick as close to the truth as possible when you're lying. Not that I'm an expert on lying or anything—nah, not me.

"So you don't like this new direction Julia wants to go in," I said.

"Not at all," Jasper sniffed. "Kid stuff. It's not art at all."

"So you probably don't care about the forgeries . . . or if her reputation is ruined."

Jasper straightened up. "Young man, her reputation is *my* reputation. We're partners. Just because I think she's learning the hard way that this is a mistake doesn't mean I want our gallery to be the victim of a forgery!"

"Since reputation is everything," I pressed, "then why did you tell Clyde Fanelli about the forgeries? That's just giving your competition ammunition."

"I did no such thing!" Jasper looked offended. "If he knows, it's because he found out some other way—maybe from that P. J. Rodriguez."

That was possible. P. J. left the gallery very angry the other day and threatened to go to Clyde Fanelli. But I couldn't see him dissing Julia that way. Was Jasper lying?

"Now if you boys will excuse me, I have some work to do." He slammed the door in my face.

Joe and I looked at each other. Joe jerked his head, and I followed him back into Julia's office. "What do you think?" he asked, shutting the door.

"I'm not sure. . . . I'd put him on the list. In the meantime, let's take a look at those frames."

The *Dark Hawk* picture still sat on the easel, with the fake Rodriguez on the floor beside it. "This one was framed by Fine Framing," I said, reading the label on the back of the *Dark Hawk* picture.

Joe bent down and picked up the Rodriguez. He flipped it to check out the back. He frowned. "This one was framed by James's Frames."

"Oh well. I guess it was too much to hope for—that they were both framed at the same place."

"I still think following up on the frame shop idea is going to yield some clues."

"Then let's go."

I pulled out my map and we located the two addresses. "Let's check out Fine Framing first," I suggested. "It's in North Beach, the Italian section. We can grab lunch there, too."

We hopped on a bus, figuring it was faster and cheaper than the cable cars. And after leaping off the last one, I liked the idea of an enclosed mode of transportation.

I knew by the smell of garlic and espresso that we were in the right neighborhood. We rang the bell and the driver let us out at the corner of a little park. People sprawled on the grass, and I heard Joe's stomach growl.

"I hope we can wrap this up quickly," he said. "I'm looking forward to a meatball sub."

I snorted. "Yeah, well, I hope we can solve this quickly so that Julia's business is saved."

"Hey, I hope that too," Joe huffed.

We walked into the store. Fancy frames hung on the walls and even from the ceiling. There was a large counter—and behind the counter was a guy who looked really familiar. He was talking on a cell phone that I'd recognize anywhere.

Metallic blue. Lightning streaks. This was the guy I saw snapping cell phone shots of the artwork at the convention!

JOE

11.
Framed?

I didn't think this was a coincidence. We see this guy secretly taking pictures on that cell phone at the convention. He's also working at one of the frame stores that had possession of one of the forged pieces of art.

I knew I shouldn't jump to conclusions, but I was excited anyway. The problem was, all we had were the dots. Now we had to connect them.

Cell Phone Dude clicked off and slipped his distinctive phone into his jeans pocket. "So, what can I do for you?"

How could I bring up the forgery? I couldn't just say, "So, have you been making fakes?" We also didn't want to tip him off till we had more information.

"I'm Joe Hardy, and this is my brother, Frank," I said, stalling to try to think of a direction to take. "And you are?"

Okay, so I sounded kind of stiff—practically Frank-ish. But I needed to know his name.

"Kyle McMartin."

"Is this your shop?" I asked.

"Nah," said Kyle. "I just work here. And speaking of work . . ." He crossed his arms over his broad chest, waiting for us to get to the point.

"We were over at PopCulture Gallery," Frank said. "I asked who did their framing and they said this place."

"Yeah, I've done stuff for them," said Kyle. "Was there something in particular that you liked? I could probably find you the same frame."

"As a matter of fact, yes," I answered, deciding to jump right into it. "There was a cool original of *Dark Hawk*. That was your frame, right?'

"Yeah. You want something like that?"

"Hey," Frank piped up. "Did you hear that it might be a forgery?"

I studied Kyle's reaction. His jaw tensed and his eyes grew darker.

"No, I didn't hear that," he said.

"Really?" I put in. "I figured it was the talk of the ComicCon. I'm sure I saw you there."

"Wasn't me," Kyle said. "And if you're not looking to place an order, I've got to get back to work. I've got a customer now."

SUSPECT PROFILE

Name: Kyle McMartin

Hometown: San Diego, moved to San Francisco to go to art school

Physical description: late twenties, muscular build, cropped black hair, lots of tattoos, has a special-looking cell phone.

Occupation: Works in a frame shop

Background: Ran with a bad crowd in high school and nearly flunked out, but his talent as an artist got him into the San Francisco Art School.

Suspicious behavior: Works in the shop where one of the forgeries was framed. Seen taking pics on his cell at the Con, even though it's against the rules. Could be how he gets the images to start working.

Suspected of: Forgery.

Possible motive: Money-school is expensive.

I turned and watched Ian Huntington come in through the door. Small world! A guy who wound up with a forged painting in the shop where the forgery was framed. I liked how things were falling into place.

"Are you two following me?" Ian joked. "You seem to be everywhere I go."

"Ian, I'm glad you're here," said Kyle. "I need you to take a look at that print you brought in. Come into the back workshop and I'll show it to you."

Ian looked confused for a moment, then shrugged. "I'm sure it's fine, but if you'd feel better if I took a look at it, sure."

"So if you'll excuse us," Kyle said pointedly.

"We were just going," I told him.

We left Fine Framing and stopped at a great-smelling Italian deli. We took our sandwiches to the park and sprawled in the sunshine.

"Did you notice how tight-lipped Kyle got when you mentioned forgeries?" I asked.

"Couldn't miss it. And he got rid of us awfully quick once Ian arrived."

"Maybe because he took the original Ian bought and copied it. He didn't want us to raise any suspicion."

I wadded up my sandwich wrapper and tossed it into the garbage can. Score!

"Do you think we should warn Ian?" Frank asked. "If Kyle is the forger, he could be doing it again with the new piece Ian brought in."

I frowned. "Julia wants us to keep this quiet. And it would blow our cover. We're not supposed to let anyone know we're on a case."

"There goes Ian now," said Frank.

Sure enough, Ian had just left the shop.

"He doesn't look happy," I observed.

"No kidding. Kyle must have screwed something up with the order."

"Speaking of . . ."

Kyle left the shop and locked it. Then he strode off in the opposite direction from Ian.

"Do you think we should follow him?" I asked.

"I don't think we have enough to go on yet," said Frank. "Let's go to the other framing store. Maybe that will help us link Kyle to both forgeries."

We tossed our soda cans into the trash bin and then hopped on a bus. James's Frames was in the Haight-Ashbury section of San Francisco.

"Wow," Frank said, peering out the bus windows. "We're in a time warp. Have we gone back to the sixties? This is hippies-ville."

"I know what you mean," I agreed, looking at the brightly painted buildings, the vintage clothing stores, and used record shops. "I feel like I should be wearing a tie-dye T-shirt."

"All that green up ahead must be Golden Gate Park," Frank said.

"There's James's Frames."

Frank pulled the cord to request a stop and we hopped off the bus. "Didn't Becky Chang say she lived in this neighborhood?" he asked.

"Yeah, I think she did," I replied.

We peered through the large glass window. I expected to see some kind of flower child behind the counter, but instead it was a woman who reminded me of Mom—if Mom was into fuchsia caftans. She didn't strike me as a forger—but I've learned that looks can be seriously deceiving.

"We need a different approach this time," I said. "You saw how quickly Kyle clammed up when we mentioned the word 'forgery.'"

"I've got an idea," said Frank. "Just follow my lead."

That didn't make me very confident, but since I couldn't come up with anything, I'd have to let Frank wing it.

"Hello there," the woman greeted us warmly. "And how may I help you?"

"I'm Frank Hardy and this is my brother, Joe," Frank said.

"I'm Melanie James," said the woman. "Very nice to meet you. Do you have some art you'd like framed? Some rock posters, maybe?"

"No, nothing like that," I said, wondering when Frank was going to take a lead for me to follow. I raised an eyebrow at him, sending him a *you can start leading anytime now, bro* message.

Frank cleared his throat. "We, uh, we inherited some paintings and they need to be framed. They've been appraised, and they're really valuable."

"How wonderful!" Melanie said. "I would be happy to work with you to give them the very best setting possible."

Frank smiled at her. "That's great. I—we—were just wondering about security. Like I said, these paintings are worth a lot of money."

Instead of getting ticked off like Kyle, this woman clucked sympathetically. "You're very wise to worry about such things. You can never be too careful."

I had to hand it to Frank—this was an excellent way to get information.

"So you're the James of James's Frames?" I asked.

The woman grinned proudly. "Yup! I started this business just a few years ago, and already I have more work than I can handle."

"Don't you have any help?" asked Frank.

Now the woman frowned. "I did. But I had to let him go."

Hmm. That meant if the forgery happened here, it was under her watch. Or she did it herself.

SUSPECT PROFILE

Name: Melanie James

Hometown: Originally San Jose, moved to San Francisco when she got married

Physical description: late forties, 5' 4", 145 lbs.; long, dark brown hair with streaks of gray, hippie-style clothing.

Occupation: Owner of James's Frames

Background: After she got divorced, she opened her own frame store to earn money and because she enjoys meeting people who like art.

Suspicious behavior: One of the forged paintings was framed at her store. Opportunity.

Suspected of: Swapping an original with a fake.

Possible motive: Money. She may have expenses now that she's divorced.

"If we brought you these paintings, how can we be assured that something won't happen to them?" I asked.

"Oh, we have an excellent security system," Melanie assured us. "Everything is locked up tight, and since I'm the only one working here, there's no confusion about the pieces."

"What if—" I wasn't sure how to bring up forgery, but she seemed pretty willing to talk, and so far hadn't taken any offense. She was rapidly getting herself erased from my suspect list. "What if someone wanted to make a forgery of the piece? Could that happen while it was getting framed?"

Her expression completely changed. Uh-oh. I must have pushed too hard. But she didn't look angry, she actually looked frightened. Was she afraid we'd found out her secret?

Then I realized that she wasn't looking at Frank or me. She was staring out the big window. I whipped my head around to see what had her so scared.

And locked eyes with Kyle McMartin.

12.
Back to School

I watched Melanie James go from helpful to freaked in a split second. I followed her gaze and saw Kyle McMartin staring into the window.

Was he angry in general, or was he ticked that we were talking to Melanie?

When he realized that all three of us were gaping at him, he took off. He ducked around a corner and out of sight.

"Are you all right?" Joe asked Melanie.

"What?" Melanie looked flustered, then smoothed back a stray hair. "Oh, yes. Sorry. I was distracted for a moment."

"You seem upset," I said. Was it because of seeing Kyle or was it our question about forgery?

She gave a little embarrassed laugh. "Really,

97

it's nothing. I—I saw someone outside. Our last encounter wasn't good."

Interesting. So she and Kyle had been at odds. "A boyfriend?" I asked, even though I doubted it highly. But it was better than asking her if it was because we had discovered she was a forger.

Now she hooted. "Oh, goodness me, no. He worked for me and I had to fire him."

"He didn't take it well, huh?" asked Joe.

"Not at all. He even harassed me for a few days. But then he stopped."

"Do you think he was here to bother you again?" I wondered how dangerous Kyle might be when crossed.

She shrugged. "I'm probably just being overly sensitive because of the hassle. He's a student at the art school nearby. He's probably in this neighborhood all the time and I've just never noticed him before."

He's probably never stopped in front of the store to gawk at the Hardys before, I thought.

"When did he work for you?" Joe asked. I could see where he was going with this. If Kyle worked at James's Frames when the *Dark Hawk* picture was copied, and then at Fine Framing in time to do the P. J. Rodriguez job, well, he'd shoot up to the top of the suspect list.

"He worked here for about two months," Melanie said. "I fired him a few weeks ago."

Bingo. The timing was just right. We finally had our first real break.

"Too bad about Kyle," she said. "He had real artistic flair. But he was just too unreliable. And if I tried to tell him that he'd done anything wrong, he'd fly off the handle."

"Where does he go to school?" Joe asked.

"San Francisco Art School. Just a few blocks over."

A little buzzer went off in my head—that's where Becky Chang and Mandy Kittson went too.

I wondered if she thought it was strange that we were asking so many questions about her former employee. But so far she just went along with us. I figured it must get lonely in that shop by herself all day, so she enjoyed the chance to talk.

"Well, we should get going. You've been really helpful," I told her. In more ways than she'd ever realize.

"Take my card," she said. "When you're ready to get those pictures of yours framed, remember James's Frames!"

"Will do!"

As we left the shop, I was already formulating a plan.

"Let's find out what kind of art Kyle was studying," I said.

"And if he was a better student than he was an employee," Joe added.

The art school was an old brick building four stories tall. We found the administrative office. The receptionist was on the phone, so I flipped through a course catalog.

"Lookie here." I held up the catalog for Joe to see. "You can major in comic-book arts."

"For real?" Joe asked.

"Can I help you?" the receptionist asked from behind the counter.

I dropped the catalog. "We wanted to know about Kyle McMartin. Can you tell me what his major is?"

"Sorry. I can't give out student information. Privacy rules."

"What's the big deal about telling us what the dude's major is?" asked Joe.

I could tell his attitude wasn't going over very well with the receptionist.

"Sorry," the woman said. "Not going to happen."

"Can we talk to the head of the comics department?" I asked, taking another route. "We're thinking of enrolling and we have some questions."

"That I can help you with," said the woman.

"There he is now, just heading up the stairs. Professor Graham. His office is one flight up, room 211."

"Thanks!" We both replied, then charged up after the professor. This place must be a pretty cool school—the teacher was wearing jeans and a T-shirt.

"Professor Graham," I called.

Professor Graham turned around. He had gray hair at his temples and wore very trendy eyeglasses. "Yes?"

"Can we ask you some questions about the program?" I asked. "We're thinking of enrolling."

"Happy to talk to fellow comics fans," he said with a smile. "I have a few minutes before my last class of the day." He ushered us into his cramped office.

I thought Chet was into comics. Every inch of this guy's office was covered in pictures, posters, and figurines. Comic books and graphic novels—and books about them—were crammed into overloaded shelves.

"Are you going to the ComicCon?" Joe asked, picking up a small statue of Mercury.

"I'm hoping to get there on the weekend," Professor Graham said. He held his hand out to Joe for the statue and then replaced it on the shelf. I guess he was the kind of guy who didn't want you touching his collection. "Are you enjoying it?"

"It's awesome," I said. "In fact, that's why we're here. We heard about your program from someone we met there. Kyle McMartin."

He raised an eyebrow. "And that made you want to come here?"

"Yeah," I said. "He said great things."

Professor Graham laughed. "Now that's a surprise. Kyle with something good to say? Doesn't sound like the Kyle I know."

"Really?" Joe said.

Professor Graham perched on the edge of his cluttered desk. "We butted heads all the time. Kyle thought he already knew everything about everything." He grinned. "Though that's true of most of my majors."

So we just confirmed that Kyle was studying comics in a serious way. "Is he good?" I asked.

Professor Graham frowned a moment, considering. "He has serious skills. Very talented. Not great with story or characters, though."

"Do you think he has a future in comics?" I asked.

Professor Graham shrugged. "Hard to say. I wanted to steer him more toward commercial design. He hand-painted his cell phone with a style that could definitely sell."

No wonder that phone of his was so distinctive. It really was one of a kind.

"Sorry I have to cut this short, guys," said Professor Graham, standing up. "I do have to get to class. If you have any questions about the program, pop me an e-mail."

"Sure thing," I said. "And thanks."

Joe and I jogged back downstairs and out into the street. I could tell my brother was pumped.

"I think we've got him!" Joe said. "He's got the skill, he's got the opportunity."

I tried not to get swept up in his enthusiasm, even though I pretty much agreed with him. Still, I didn't want us to get ahead of ourselves. "Okay, but what about motive?"

"What *about* motive?" Joe asked. "Money, money, and then some more of that money."

"It *would* be all profit," I mused, starting to walk back toward the bus stop. "All he'd have to do is shell out for supplies, and that would be it. But why go to all the trouble of stealing the originals and then switching them for the fakes and returning them? That's a lot of risk. Why not just make the forged ones and leave the originals alone?"

"You heard Julia—you can't every get detail unless you see the drawings up close and personal."

I nodded. "Becky said the same thing."

"Besides, Julia is selling to private collectors. Once the pics are hanging in someone's living room, they're out of sight. At that point, who's going to identify it as a fake? All the paperwork on authenticity was already done."

I could see where he was heading with this. "But a new buyer might want it checked out, so he'd need the real deal."

Joe frowned. "But isn't it kind of a small world? Don't all the collectors know what's in each other's collections? There are rumors and gossip about everything."

"About the artists and the comics themselves," I pointed out. "Not the collectors. And if he sold overseas, maybe to someone who didn't check too carefully . . ."

I stopped when I realized we were passing the art supply store. The one where P. J. Rodriguez bought his special sketch pads.

"This should clinch it," I said, pulling open the door. "If Kyle McMartin buys the same pads . . ."

"We get to hang at the Con, no strings—or cases—attached!" Joe finished for me.

The store was a ramshackle, messy place full of everything an artist of any type would need—and lots of items I couldn't identify. We checked the store directory and found the paper and sketch-books.

As soon as I saw the girl behind the counter, I knew exactly what was about to happen. Joe was going to go into immediate flirt mode.

"I bet you hear this all the time," he said, leaning on the counter. "But you are the best work of art in the place."

Way to be predictable.

The girl giggled. "Actually, no. I've never heard that particular line."

"Well, I can see why my bud Kyle McMartin never mentioned you. He's in here all the time. And I bet you're the reason why."

"I don't know any Kyle," the girl said, eating up my brother's every word.

Watching Joe made me wonder if I'd be able to eat at all. Totally barf-worthy behavior. I couldn't believe it was actually working.

"You may not know him by name, but he buys some special paper from you."

"Oh, yeah?" said the girl. "Which?"

Hmm. This could be a problem. We never found out what the stuff was called.

"The same kind P. J. Rodriguez uses. Kyle is way into comics, so he likes to use the same stuff his art hero does."

"We wanted some of that paper too," I said, trying to move this along. "So can you check it for us?"

"And I'm sure you'll find Kyle's name as one of your best customers. But now that I've met you, I'm going to compete for that spot."

The girl giggled again and started punching things into the computer. "Well, Kyle does buy a lot from us, but I'm not seeing any special sort of paper. Just an assortment of pretty standard stuff."

My forehead furrowed. "Can you check P. J. Rodriguez's orders? We do want to know what that paper is."

"Sure." The girl clicked again. "Here it is. Oh, sorry." She gave Joe a pout. "I can't sell you any."

"P. J. bought the last of it?" Joe asked.

"No, a girl with an art student discount. She's the only other local person who buys it. Becky Chang."

13.
Paper Trail

"Well . . . isn't that interesting," I said, trying to cover how stunned I was. I'd been so completely sure that Kyle was the person who made that Rodriguez copy that it never occurred to me that any other name would pop up in the computer.

Did I have to totally rethink the suspect list? Dang! And I thought we had this one nailed.

"I also have a lot of online orders for this paper," the salesgirl said. "We have shipments that go out all over the place. Pretty cool, huh?"

She shot me a winning smile. Dimples. Gets me every time. Only I couldn't stay and chat—at least not with her. Becky was now the girl we had to talk to.

My cell chimed. "Hang on," I said to the girl. I checked the number. Chet.

"I think we're late," I told Frank. " 'Sup, dude?" I said into the phone. "Meet any superheroes?"

"I thought we were going to meet out front," said Chet. "Did I get that wrong?"

SUSPECT PROFILE

<u>Name:</u> Becky Chang

<u>Hometown:</u> San Francisco

<u>Physical description:</u> 19 years old, 5'5", 120 lbs., goth attire and makeup, blue streaks in her jet-black hair.

<u>Occupation:</u> Art student

<u>Background:</u> Has always wanted to draw comics, contributed artwork to high school papers, a huge fan. Very driven to succeed in comics.

<u>Suspicious behavior:</u> Allegedly cheated at school by swiping Mandy's senior proposal, studies the art very closely at the Con, buys the same specialty paper used in the latest fake.

<u>Motive:</u> Money? Ambition?

"No, man," I told him. "We just ended up checking out Haight-Ashbury, and it was farther away than we realized."

We made plans to meet for dinner back at the pier near our hotel.

"So you don't want to buy anything?" the girl asked.

"No, thanks," said Frank.

"Another time," I added.

Didn't want to make her feel bad.

The pier was crowded again with tourists and convention-goers. I looked around for Becky but didn't see her. She seemed to be the most likely choice for that Rodriguez fake. Did that mean she was behind the other forgeries, too? That scenario got my vote. Still, I couldn't shake the feeling that Kyle was into this up to his tattooed neck.

Chet waved us over from a table overlooking the water. This was the life: burgers on the pier, perfect weather—closing in on a suspect.

"We've got to stop meeting like this," Ian joked, clamping a pudgy hand on my shoulder.

"I keep running into people too," said Chet. "I think a lot of the people at the con hang here at Fisherman's Wharf."

"It really is more for tourists than for locals

like me," Ian said. "But I have a boat at the nearby marina, and it's a good place for meetings with like-minded comics fans like you boys."

"Did you hang at the con all day?" Chet asked. "I did."

"No," Ian said. "I had a few appointments. Which reminds me. What were you two doing at the frame store?"

Think fast.

Frank thought faster. "Julia asked us to find out their return policy. When you brought back that drawing, you'd had it reframed."

Good cover.

"Oh that's right!" Ian said. "I'm so sorry. I tried putting it in a new frame to see if that would help make it look better at home. I'll bring the original one back."

"Don't worry about it," Frank assured him. "Julia didn't mind."

"So you and Kyle have worked together before, huh?" I asked. Just because Becky was now also a suspect didn't put Kyle in the clear. In fact, the two could be working together. "What do you think of him?"

Ian looked surprised. "Why?"

"Oh, well, we heard that he got fired from his

last job," I said. "So we were kind of wondering about what your experience with him has been like—and with that shop."

"For Julia's sake," Frank added. Smartly, I have to admit. "She does a lot of framing."

"You know more than I do about Kyle," said Ian. "What else have you learned?"

"Did you guys hear that there might be forgeries of some of the comic-book art at the con?" Chet asked. "Maybe that's why your guy was fired."

Some days Chet is just too smart for *our* own good.

"Forgeries?" Ian repeated, incredulous. "Who's been talking about forgeries?"

Chet shrugged. "Some random people were talking about it. I don't know their names."

I could totally kick myself. And my brother. We should have clued Chet in—at least as much as we could. That way he would have kept his mouth shut about the rumors.

Our best friend was our client's worst enemy. He was telling exactly the wrong guy about Julia's problems: her biggest buyer.

We were brought in so that this could be kept totally quiet. And now Chet was making a whole lot of noise.

14.
Keeping Secrets, Part Two

"You know," Chet said, "I think I heard it from that guy who owns that shop Monsters and Heroes."

"Do you think Kyle had something to do with this?" Ian demanded. "Is that why you're asking questions about him?"

I hate it when someone asks me a direct question and all I can do is lie. Directly.

"We really just wanted to know if that's a frame shop Julia should use," I said. "I haven't heard any rumors. Have you, Joe?"

When in doubt, get backup.

"Nah. Well, I heard a rumor that Scotty Milner is thinking about switching publishers."

Wow. Joe was paying attention. I hadn't heard that.

"That's old news," Chet scoffed. "Every time he has something new, that rumor goes around."

"But nothing about Kyle?" Ian persisted.

I had to get him off this topic. "I heard a rumor about a total dork who busted in on some actors trying to re-enact a scene from the new Mercury movie."

Chet's eyes widened. "No way!"

I nodded, ignoring the daggers Joe was sending me. "Way. And that brilliant dweeb was none other than . . ." I played a drumroll on the table with my fork. "My brother, Joe Hardy!"

Chet burst out laughing. "Oh, man. I wish I had been there."

Ian fiddled with the change in his pocket, but I think he realized we were onto other stuff. Like making fun of Joe. Typical teenage fun—and not where he wanted the conversation to go. But we were unstoppable.

"There were plenty of people snapping pix. I just hope it shows up in heavy rotation on the Internet!"

"Would you guys quit it?" Joe complained. "I really don't want a replay of my humiliation."

All for the cause, bro, I thought. *Ian is losing interest.*

"Well," he said. "I see my dinner companion waving. I expect I'll see you at the con again tomorrow."

"You bet!" said Chet.

Ian trundled away.

"So did the actors get totally ticked off?" Chet asked.

P. J. Rodriguez suddenly plopped down beside me. "Did you have any luck?"

Chet dropped his fork. He gaped at P. J., his eyes huge.

"We're still looking into it," I said, hoping this would be enough to satisfy him. This was not a conversation to have with Chet sitting right there.

P. J. looked disappointed. Which is probably why Joe added, "But we think we have a lead."

Now Chet gaped at Joe. Then at me. Clearly his mind was getting blown right about now.

P. J. nodded. "I know you guys are doing your best. It's just so frustrating."

"Tell me about it," I said. As frustrating as trying to keep Chet in the dark.

"Gotta go," P. J. said. "Got some peeps waiting."

The whole time I watched him slouch away I could feel Chet's eyes boring into the back of my skull.

Time to face the music.

Chet's mouth was still hanging open. Any minute a fly was going to buzz right in.

He blinked a few times, then said, "You didn't *tell* me?"

I could tell he was pretty peeved. "We—"

"You know P. J. Rodriguez, my main man, and you don't *tell* me?"

Oh! He was stunned by our palling around with P. J., not that we were on a case.

"*And* you're on a *case*?" he demanded.

Okay, so I came to a conclusion a bit too quickly.

Joe and I exchanged a look. Only his was a bit too cryptic for me to read.

Chet's eyes narrowed. "Is this birthday present legit or are we out here because you're on a case?"

Ouch! The last thing I wanted was for Chet to feel badly—or cheated out of his birthday present. What do we do?

"This is totally for you," Joe assured him. "The whole plan, the surprise, everything. It's just that—"

"We got wind of the forgeries and offered to help. That's all," I said. "Strictly accidental—"

"Amateur," Joe added.

"Accidental amateur detecting," I finished.

In other words, we lied.

15.
Monsters and Heroes

That cat got let out of the bag, all right. But we were staying in the same hotel room and attending the same convention. I'm surprised we kept the secret this long.

"So is the rumor true?" Chet asked. "Are there really forgeries being sold at the convention?"

I glanced at Frank. We had to be careful about how much we let Chet know, but he could be useful as an extra set of eyes and ears at the con. He hears all the gossip and knows a lot of inside information. Frank must have been thinking the same thing, because he gave a little nod.

"Julia discovered that two of her drawings are fake—the *Dark Hawk* and one by P. J. that Ian had bought. But Ian doesn't know anything about it."

"Till now," Frank said.

"Sorry, guys," Chet said. "But this should teach you not to keep things from me. If I knew you were on a case, I never would have said anything,"

"We know," I said. "And it has to stay that way."

"We promised Julia we'd keep it a secret until she figured out how it happened and who did it," said Frank.

"With your help, of course," Chet said with a grin.

"Strictly amateur," Frank emphasized. "We'll do the best we can."

"I wonder why Ian was so interested in the forgeries and Kyle," I said.

Chet snorted. "Duh. Because if Julia is selling forgeries, everything he owns could be a fake. He'd have a totally worthless collection."

Exactly what Julia was afraid of. That if news got out, everything she has ever sold would be called into question.

"This could really explode in Julia's face," Frank said.

"Was that what P. J. was asking about?" asked Chet.

"Sort of," I said. "Someone left a perfect copy of one of his drawings at Julia's booth. He wanted us to find out who would do that—and why."

"I wish *I* could draw a perfect copy of one of P. J.'s drawings," Chet said.

"Hey, there's Kyle now," said Frank.

I turned and sure enough, there was Kyle, chatting away with Clyde Fanelli. Interesting. Clyde would be thrilled if Julia's gallery went under. Could they be working together? But where did that leave Becky and the mystery of the rare sketch pad paper?

"Monsters and Heroes has some really cool stuff," Chet said. "But it's way out of my price range."

Kyle and Clyde didn't look very chummy. Maybe something was going wrong with their scheming. Something like ATAC agents on the case.

"Some guy came in and returned something he bought," Chet continued. "Clyde was kind of peeved."

"Was it Ian?" I asked, wondering if this was something he did all over town.

"Nah. Some guy named Mark. I hoped it would make Clyde bring the price down, but no such luck."

Interesting. Julia was right. This indecisiveness seemed to go with the art collector territory.

Kyle and Clyde parted ways. Kyle slipped off into the crowd, and Clyde headed our way. When he passed the table, I called his name.

SUSPECT PROFILE

Name: Clyde Fanelli

Hometown: San Francisco

Physical description: Age 34, 5'10", 185 lbs., heavily muscled like a weight lifter, buzz cut.

Occupation: Owner of Monsters and Heroes Gallery

Background: Worked in many businesses, often fired. Investigated for shady business practices in his last venture, an online auction service, but nothing was proved.

Suspicious behavior: Spreading the word about the forgery, lots of contact with Kyle, chatting up the artists Julia represents.

Suspected of: Working with an artist to make forgeries.

Possible motive: Beat the competition. If Julia's reputation is ruined, the artists will go to him instead.

He glanced around, and I waved him over. "Our friend Chet here loves the stuff you carry," I told him, figuring flattery was a good place to start.

119

"It's awesome," Chet gushed. "That saber you have from the film version of *The Dungeon of Desperadoes* is amazing. And the first editions!" Chet let out a whistle. "Choice!"

"Glad you appreciate my shop," said Clyde. "Stop by—and buy!"

"I wish . . ." Chet sighed.

"Say," I said, hoping to sound casual. "That guy you were talking to. What's his name? He looks familiar."

"We think maybe we know him from back home," Frank added, improving the cover story.

"Kyle?" Clyde said. "I doubt it. He's local. He works at a frame shop."

"Oh?" said Frank.

"I hope he's not a friend of yours," Clyde added. "I had to chew him out. He's late with an important delivery."

"Something for the convention?" asked Chet eagerly.

"You'll have to keep stopping by the booth to find out," Clyde answered with a slick salesman's grin. "See you at the con."

"Oh man, he's going over to sit with Scotty Milner," Chet said, watching Clyde weave through the tables. "I wish I had the nerve to introduce myself."

"Maybe you will by the end of the convention," Frank told him.

Maybe by then Clyde Fanelli will be Scotty Milner's official representative, I thought. I was certain Clyde would tell Scotty all about the forgeries.

Forgeries that he might have hired Kyle to do.

16.
Pretty Sketchy

Could the work Kyle was late delivering be another forgery? Just because Clyde didn't seem to like the guy didn't mean they weren't working together.

We still had to figure out how Becky played into all this. That paper was pretty incriminating, though I guess someone could have ordered it online and then dropped the forged drawing off at Julia's booth. The person could have been from anywhere.

Instead of narrowing things down, it seemed like our list just kept expanding.

Clyde and Scotty looked pretty cozy. On second look, Clyde was basically sucking up to Scotty, and Scotty was basking in the adoration.

Maybe Chet didn't want to meet his idol. He could wind up disappointed.

We dropped the forgery conversation and finished dinner. "So what now?" Chet asked.

I wadded up my napkin and tossed it onto my plate. "It's going to be light for a while longer. We could head over to the marina and maybe join a game of soccer or Frisbee or something."

"Sounds cool," said Joe.

After paying the check, we wandered through the crowds at the pier. The weather was turning a bit chilly, as the trademark San Francisco fog began to roll in. The island of Alcatraz, home at one time to a notorious prison, was barely visible in the soft gray clouds.

Mixed in with the carousel music, the crowds, and the music from the open restaurants, I heard strange barking sounds. Weird. It didn't sound like a pack of dogs. And what would a pack of dogs be doing on a pier?

"What's that?" I asked.

"I read in one of the guidebooks that there are sea lions around here somewhere," Chet said.

I remembered an aquarium on the map, but the barking didn't seem like it was coming from that direction.

Joe nudged me. "There's someone we need to say hello to."

"I recognize those blue streaks," I said. Time to

talk to Becky about the specialty paper and the latest P. J. Rodriguez fake.

Becky sat on a bench overlooking the water with her back to us. Good. I wanted to see what she was drawing.

As we got closer, I realized the barking sound was coming from just below us. We were on the second level of the pier. I could see tips of sails bobbing in the water below us. Could that be what Becky was drawing?

"Let's surprise her," I told Chet. I didn't want him alerting her. I wanted to see if I could get a quick look at her sketch pad. She was concentrating hard—people milled all around her and she never glanced up. Excellent.

Joe and I sidled up on either side of her. I peeked over her shoulder.

Yowza. My eyes bugged. First of all, it was that same specialty sketch pad P. J. uses. Second of all—

"Hey, that's really good!" Chet exclaimed. "It looks exactly like that new P. J. Rodriguez character, Flint."

Exactly.

Startled, Becky whirled around on the bench and shut her notebook. She recovered quickly and plastered a great big dark purple smile on her face.

"Hi, guys!" she said.

"You're really good at drawing comics," said Chet. "Did you hear that the Flint series is due out in two months?"

While Chet and Becky talked about Flint, I scanned the cover of her sketch pad. My big eyes got bigger.

P. J. Rodriguez's schedule at the con. His appearances at Julia's booth, his panels, and his address. She was either the biggest fan ever or a stalker.

Or a forger with an agenda.

"What else are you drawing?" Joe asked, reaching for the sketch pad.

She yanked the pad out of his reach and clutched it to her chest. "That's private," she said.

"You have that same special paper that P. J. uses," I pointed out. "Not too many people have that."

Becky looked uncomfortable. "Yeah, so?"

"Have you heard the rumors about forgeries at the convention?" asked Joe.

I wasn't sure if my brother was taking the right approach. On the one hand—good. Push the issue. On the other—if she wasn't the forger, did we really want to spread that news around?

Becky rolled her eyes. "Rumors. There are always rumors about everything at the cons."

"Yeah, but did you know that the forger sent P. J. one of his own pictures?" Joe pressed.

"Talk about obnoxious," I added.

A horrified look crossed Becky's face. We'd hit a nerve. Excellent.

"Since you're so good at copying," I said, "and happen to have the exact same kind of very special paper—"

Before I could finish, Becky took off running.

I ask you: Does an innocent person run?

I spotted her dyed hair bobbing in between people along the concrete wall of the balcony. We caught up to her easily—a tourist joint is a good place to get lost in a crowd, but not a good place to try to make a quick getaway.

Joe reached her first. He grabbed her arm. "So what else do you have in that sketch pad?" he demanded.

Becky jerked violently, pulling herself free of him and sending him slamming into the low wall.

SPLASH!

Uh-oh.

Make that slamming him *over* the wall!

17.

Swimming with Sea Lions

Ye-ah! This water is *cold!*

The cold shot through me like a jolt of lightning. My chest tightened from the temperature and the shock of plunging into the bay.

I kicked my feet hard and shot back up to the surface. I broke through and gasped for air,

It all happened so fast. One minute I was grabbing Becky and her sketch pad. The next it was up and over and into the water!

Water streamed into my eyes as I did a quick scan. Blinking hard, I was relieved to see that there weren't any boats or Jet Skis around. All clear. Nothing but several floating docks.

My clothes weighed me down a bit, so I couldn't get too high up above the surface. I needed to get

127

to one of those docks fast. I didn't want my jeans and shoes to drag me under. And they were getting heavier by the second.

I was wearing high-tops, so I couldn't just kick them off. Instead I put major oomph into my butterfly kick and made it to the bobbing dock in just a few strokes.

I really felt the extra weight of soaked jeans, hoodie, and wet canvas sneakers as I pressed my palms hard onto the dock. The dock tipped toward me as I pushed up. It then suddenly tipped sharply in the other direction.

Huh?

A big, ugly snout appeared and the creature let out a loud bark.

"Yah!" I yelped, and flung myself back into the water.

So, all that barking I heard really was the famous Pier 39 sea lions!

I treaded water, trying to come up with a plan. And I had to come up with one fast—wet jeans weigh a ton.

I heard a loud splash, and then something bumped my butt! Hard!

The force of the sea lion's shove flopped me forward. I jerked my head back up, spitting out a mouthful of water.

Another sea lion lumbered to the edge of the floating dock and rolled into the water. Before I could book out of there, it shoved its huge snout into my chest. I dunked back under water.

These guys were playing catch—and I was the ball!

I had to get out of there pronto!

My leg muscles burned as I fought against the weight of my jeans, my shoes, and the water. I could see dozens of sea lions sunning themselves on the floating docks off to my right—so I swam left.

I put power into every stroke, cutting through the water as best I could despite my wet clothing. I wanted distance between me and the sea lions. I could still hear barking behind me, but I didn't waste any effort looking back. Luckily, the intensity of my movements kept my muscles warm, and the chilly water wasn't freezing them up.

In a few minutes I clambered up onto a deserted floating platform. I wanted to put up a big sign: NO SEA LIONS ALLOWED! PEOPLE ONLY!

I lay gasping on the boards, which were still warm from the sun. But the sun was going down, and I knew that any minute I'd be shivering.

I rolled over, pushed myself up to standing, and gazed around.

Hundreds of eyes gazed back at me.

Tourists of every description watched the whole thing. Some waved, some applauded, some laughed, and lots were snapping pictures.

Great.

"What do you think you're doing?" an angry voice demanded.

I turned to see a guy speeding toward me in a little boat, its engine roaring. I had a feeling that if he could, the guy would be roaring too.

"Get in," he ordered.

"Hey, man," I said, navigating the tricky move from the floating dock into the equally unsteady motorboat. "That was a total accident."

Water dripped down the back of my neck, from my jeans, and out of my shoes. The boat zoomed around the side of the pier. We were moving at a fast clip, and the breeze it created chilled me. San Francisco may be in sunny California, but you wouldn't know it right now.

"There's a stiff fine for bothering the sea lions," the guy told me.

"They were the ones bothering *me*!" I protested. "If you had seen any of that, you'd know I got away from them as fast as I could!"

"How'd you end up in the water?" asked the guy. He was wearing some sort of official-looking windbreaker. I guessed he was either the pier police or the sea lions' personal bodyguards. I could tell he'd have no sense of humor about this. "Some friends dare you? Showing off for a girl?"

Actually, those sounded like a lot better answers than the truth. "I told you—it was an accident. I slipped and went over the railing."

"That'll teach you to run on the pier," the guy grumbled.

"Oh, I learned my lesson, sir." Time to play the contrite, apologetic dweeb. I wanted to avoid that stiff fine! "It will never happen again."

I hoped that was true. It was no fun getting up close and personal with a sea lion—or being knocked around by him and his whiskered friends!

What is it with me and animals lately? Elephants? Sea lions? If this kept up I might end up as some buffalo's soccer ball!

It could happen. I read in a guidebook that there are buffalo in Golden Gate Park!

"Well . . ." The guy scrutinized me from under his bushy, sun-bleached eyebrows. I put on my most innocent face. The one that makes Frank gag.

"Okay, I'll let you off with a warning. This time." He pulled up in front of a wooden ladder out of view of the public. It led up to the main level of the pier, behind offices.

"Thanks," I said. "I appreciate it." I gripped the wooden rung and lifted myself out of the boat. I climbed back up onto the pier.

That's when I realized that Becky's sketch pad—aka possible evidence—was now at the bottom of the bay. Maybe a sea lion was going to snack on it.

I slogged my way back to where I'd so dramatically left the balcony. My sneakers squished the entire way. I was getting colder and clammier by the minute.

The only good news was that Becky was flanked by Chet and Frank. We'd still be able to question her.

"That was some dive," Frank said. "You okay?"

I nodded, spraying water. "I was almost a foosball for a pair of sea lions, but I'm fine."

"My sketch pad!" Becky wailed. "You knocked it right into the water!"

"Hey!" I snapped. "You knocked *me* right into the water. To me that's the bigger deal."

Becky crossed her arms over her chest and pouted. "And I don't see why these goons think they can keep me hanging here."

"Didn't you want to find out if I survived?" I asked sarcastically. "Or are you in too much of a hurry to copy some more of P. J. Rodriguez's drawings?"

Becky looked stunned. Her mouth opened and closed a few times like a fish.

"That was you, wasn't it?" I went on, stepping right up into her face. I was dripping mad. "You're the one who left that drawing for P. J. at the Pop-Culture booth."

"You know about that?" asked Becky.

"Heard it from P. J. himself," Frank said.

Now her eyes opened really big, and she got this weird look on her face. I thought maybe she'd faint. "Did he like it?" she asked in a breathy, slightly hysterical tone.

"Like it?" I repeated. "It made him furious!"

"Wh-what?" Becky stumbled backward slightly, as if my words nearly knocked her over.

"How would you feel," Frank said, "to have your work copied and then have the forger taunt you with your own drawing?"

"F-forger?" Becky stammered. "No! that's not— I would never—"

She burst into tears.

It is not a pretty sight when a girl who's into the whole goth look starts crying. Black and purple streaks ran down her face.

"I would never do anything to hurt P. J.," she wailed. "He's my idol. I love him!"

Frank and I looked at each other. He raised an eyebrow. I shrugged.

"So you wanted him to see you were an artist?" Chet asked gently. "Just like him."

Becky nodded and gazed at Chet with grateful raccoon eyes. "It was my way to honor him. Show him how much his work means to me."

Chet fished around for a pack of tissues and handed them to Becky. "I heard that's how Phil Kenton got into the biz. He sent Tasha King a copy he made from one of her comics."

Becky nodded. "I heard that too." She made little sniveling sounds while I did some thinking.

Chet seemed to buy her story. Maybe she thought this was a way to her big break. From what I'd seen so far, fans did all kinds of things that seemed over the top.

But if what Mandy told us was true, Becky didn't mind cheating if it suited her. So she had no problem with the concept. She had the skill, but did she do the deed? As far as we knew, she never had the opportunity to switch the originals for the fakes. We'd still have to find out more.

I shoved my hands into my armpits, trying to warm them. I had a full body shudder. Wet clothes are not comfy.

Frank glanced my way. "We gotta get this guy into dry gear," he said.

"I'm f-f-fine," I chattered.

"Dude. Your lips are blue," he said.

Becky wiped her face and stood. "So I can go now?" Now that she wasn't crying anymore, she was back to having attitude. Blue lips were no concern to her—she paints her own that color, on purpose!

"Sure," I said.

"Are you going to warn me not to leave town like they do on TV?" She smirked.

"We know you won't." I smirked back. "There are still two more days left of the convention."

Becky flounced away.

"Okay, I'm officially freezing now," I announced. "Can we get out of here?"

Most of the crowd who'd seen my amazing swim with the sea lions had gone, so at least I didn't have to endure any teasing. I did get some weird looks, though. I guess most people don't walk along the pier soaking wet and shivering.

Frank nudged me. "Look who Becky happens to be talking to."

I looked. "Kyle McMartin."

"The guy you were talking to Ian about?" Chet asked.

"The very same," I said.

"That guy sure gets around," Frank commented, watching Becky leave and Clyde Fanelli approach Kyle. "He seems to know everybody!"

"Maybe we're not dealing with a single forger," I suggested. "Maybe it's some kind of forgery ring."

"Good thing Ian brought in that fake," said Frank. "I have a feeling that frame has turned out to be a really crucial clue."

"I'm sorry, Kyle isn't working today." The girl behind the counter at Fine Framing smiled. "Is there something I can help you with?"

Frank and I decided to skip the convention today. We wanted to close in on Kyle and find out if we were on the right track. I could feel it in my bones that we were. Only we needed more than my bones to bring Kyle to justice.

"We were supposed to pick up something from him," Frank said. "Can we go in the back and find it?"

Long shot. Somehow I didn't think she'd go for it.

We had hoped to find a way to get into the back room, see if that's where Kyle might be making forgeries—or even storing the originals.

"What's your name? I'll see if your order is ready."

"It's not an order," I said quickly. "It's, uh, a bag. Kyle accidentally took mine and he said he'd leave it here for me." I hoped I'd picked something that she'd let me go find on my own.

"Sorry, that's off-limits to anyone but employees," the girl told us. "I didn't see a bag back there, though. Maybe he took it to his studio?"

"You know, you may be right," said Frank. "I think that *is* what he said. But I didn't bring the address."

"It's right nearby," the girl said. "It's all artists renting studio space. It's a really cool place. If you do large canvases you get the upper floors, if you do digital stuff they can hook you up with Wi-Fi. I'm saving up to rent a space there myself."

"It's pricey?" Joe asked.

The girl nodded. "But so worth it. I don't want my paint stinking up my apartment."

She gave us the address. It was right near one of the entrances to Golden Gate Park.

We headed toward the line of trees, and the minute we turned a corner I spotted Kyle up ahead waiting for the light to change. He was carrying a laptop and yakking a mile a minute on that very snazzy cell.

I grabbed Joe's arm and yanked him into a doorway.

"We don't want him to see us," I hissed.

"He's probably heading right for that studio," Joe whispered. "We can surprise him there."

We waited a few minutes to put some distance between us and Kyle. Then we found the studio building.

Piece o' cake. The door was wide open.

I spotted a list of "rules" posted in the vestibule. "This is cool," I said, scanning the list. "Each studio locks, the building has twenty-four-hour access."

"If Kyle is making forgeries, this would be a perfect place to do it," said Joe. "It's private, it's near where he lives, it's near the frame shop. . . ."

"So let's find out!"

The girl at the frame store had described where Kyle's private studio was—second floor, three doors down.

Too bad it was the door that was padlocked.

"We must have missed him," I said.

"If this was where he was headed," said Joe.

We tromped back down the stairs. A man was out front, putting out trash. "Do you know Kyle McMartin?" I asked him.

"Yeah," the man said, rubbing a handkerchief over his sweating forehead.

"Was he here?" I asked.

The man nodded. "He dropped off a laptop, but he went back out again."

"Thanks," I said. "We'll try back later."

"Well, that was a bust," said Joe.

I felt the same frustration.

Now what?

"Let's kill time in the park," Joe suggested. "We can keep checking back."

"He may not *be* back," I reminded him.

"You have a better plan?"

Not really. "Okay. But we'll avoid the lakes. Don't want you to wind up soaking wet again."

"Ha, ha."

We entered the park, and the first thing I noticed was how quiet it was. We quickly found ourselves in a deeply wooded area. Cool to think this was just a few blocks from busy city streets.

Cool until I got the very definite sense that Joe and I weren't alone.

We were being followed.

18.
Bad Odds

The back of my neck tingled.

"You feel that?" I asked Frank.

"Like we're being followed?" he replied.

"Exactly." It's weird what that feels like. There's kind of a shadow, a cloud, lurking just out of sight. My stalker-sense has never failed me yet.

"Let's lose 'em," said Frank. He took off running.

Our feet pounded the asphalt, and I heard thundering footfalls behind us. How many of them were there? They obviously didn't care that we knew they were following us.

My lungs felt like they were burning as we raced through the unfamiliar park. Park? This was more like the deep woods!

Make that *dark* woods. The overcast day was

why there weren't people around. It had been threatening to rain all morning.

I risked a glance back. It was Kyle—and two brutal-looking thug types. They were several yards back, but they were keeping up.

And they probably knew this park a lot better than we did.

"How do we lose them?" I panted.

"Don't think we will," Frank huffed back. "Maybe we should confront them."

I slowed to a jog. "You're right. This may be our best shot at finding out about the forgeries."

The guys ran up to us and stopped.

"Hey, Kyle," I called. "You didn't strike me as the jogger type. Out for an afternoon run?"

"Why have you been asking people about me?" Kyle growled.

"You're an interesting character," I said. "We wanted to get to know you better."

Wap! My head whipped sharply to the side as one of the thugs connected with my face.

I did *not* see that coming!

"Back off," snarled Frank. He was in a strong fighter's pose: hands up in fists, feet wide for stability. "You have questions, so do we."

"I don't care if you have questions," Kyle said. "What I want is for you to get off my case."

I rubbed my face where the punch had landed. "You have something to hide, McMartin?"

"What I've got is none of your business," Kyle retorted.

This time I was ready. I blocked the thug's hit—and landed one of my own.

The three-against-two ratio wasn't working for us. I had no doubt we could take them if there were only the two thugs. But with Kyle in the mix, it was hard.

While Frank was duking it out with Thug One and Kyle, I had my hands full with Thug Two. I was a lot faster than he was, so I could duck and weave. But he was bigger and packed serious weight behind each punch.

Sweat stung my eyes, blinding me for a moment. *Wham.* A pop right in the mouth. I tasted salt and knew my lip was split. I rebalanced by going into a deep lunge and then knocked my opponent's jaw with the tip of my foot.

My karate teacher would have been proud.

Thug Two's head snapped back and he toppled over backward, landing with a satisfying grunt. I took my split-second opportunity and charged at Kyle.

Frank didn't have a chance—it was two against one. Thug One had somehow gotten the advantage and was now holding my brother's arms while Kyle pummeled him.

Frank struggled, the veins in his arms popping with effort, his muscles straining against Thug One's grip. But the dude was massive, and Frank couldn't break free.

I hurled myself at Kyle, knocking him to the ground. We squirmed, each of us trying to get the advantage. I grappled with him, thrust my shoulder sharply up under his jaw. He let go, and I managed to roll away and leap back onto him—all before he could regroup.

"Now you answer *our* questions," I shouted at Kyle, pinning him to the ground.

Ewwwwwww! Dude spit at me! Right in the face!

I didn't dare wipe off the slobber. I didn't want to give him a chance to knock me back down.

A pair of massive beefy paws gripped my shoulders and pulled me off Kyle.

Dang. I forgot for a minute about the extra thug.

Only he didn't hit me. Instead, he helped Kyle up.

"Gotta book," he told Kyle. "Badges en route."

Thug One released Frank, who crumpled to the ground. Our three assailants took off running.

Now I saw why—way up ahead a park security

cruiser turned onto a path leading straight toward us.

Kyle stopped and faced us. "Consider this a warning," he shouted. Then he spun around and vanished into the woods.

I dropped down beside Frank. Man, he looked bad. There was a cut above his eye and blood was coming out of his nose. He was covered in dirt and grass, and he was seriously pale.

"You okay?" I asked.

Frank let out a groan as he straightened up to sit. He nodded, but he didn't say anything. He took in slow, deep breaths.

"We totally would've had them," I said. "Even if that security car hadn't shown up."

The car approached, and I looked at Frank. "Should we report them?"

"Nah," Frank said, color returning to his face. "They're long gone." He looked at me. "Do I look as bad as you?"

"Depends. How bad do I look?"

Slowly we managed to get up and checked our aches and pains. Frank's nose wasn't actually broken, and the punches Kyle landed hadn't hit anything supercritical. He was just banged up and sore.

I was going to have a major shiner and some

bruising, but nothing more serious than that. A rough day snowboarding sometimes resulted in worse.

"That clinches it for me," I said. "Kyle is totally the bad guy. He's had the opportunity and skills. This little *warning*"—I made air quotes with my fingers—"just proves that he has major secrets to hide."

"We still have no proof. It's just not enough to bring him in," Frank argued.

I frowned. Okay, maybe I even pouted. I was so certain of this. But Frank was right. We had to get the actual evidence.

"You know," said Frank, nodding his head the way he sometimes does when he's thinking, "if I remember right, those studios were more like cubicles. Temporary-type walls like you'd see in an office."

"Your point?" I asked.

"I don't think the walls went all the way up to the ceilings."

I thought back. He was right. "Makes sense," I said. "Otherwise the fumes from the paint couldn't escape, and the artists would pass out."

I started to head back toward the exit, but Frank stopped me.

"Dude. No offense, but we really shouldn't

be allowed out in the general population looking like this."

We were totally gunked up with dirt, grass, and blood. No one was going to talk to us—or even let us into the building—looking like this.

"Let's see if we can find a place to clean up here," he said. "I don't want to even get on a bus like this."

We found a restroom and washed off the blood and did what we could with the dirt. My T-shirt was going to be grass-stained for good. Aunt Trudy had been trying to get me to toss it for weeks now. What did I care about a couple of holes? Now she was going to get her way.

I raked my wet fingers through my hair. "Presentable?" I asked Frank.

"Close enough. How about me?"

"Well, you've never been *presentable*, but you'll do."

"I'd hit you, but my fists hurt."

We walked out of the park a lot more slowly than we had walked in. Some of the places I got hit throbbed, and pretty much every muscle ached. I was going to nail Kyle for this. I didn't need any more convincing.

We arrived at the artists' studio building and climbed the stairs to the second floor.

"So are we hoping that he's here or that he's not?" asked Frank.

"What do we do if he's here?" I said. I didn't want another run-in—I was hurting as it was, and Frank was way worse.

Frank sighed. "We deal with that if it happens. I think we can't wait. My guess is he came after us because he thinks we're onto him. If that's the case, he'll get rid of the evidence ASAP."

"True." I just wasn't sure how easily either of us would climb up and over the wall and drop down into Kyle's studio.

"Uh-oh. Looks like someone's home," I said, noticing that Kyle's studio door was open.

"This time, we've got the benefit of surprise."

"And maybe this time the odds will favor us," I said. "If he's in there alone, we can let him see how not nice it is to gang up."

We snuck up to the side of the doorway. I listened and heard nothing. Good. That meant he was alone.

"Hey, Kyle," I called, stepping into the open doorway. "We just remembered a few questions—"

I stopped dead in my tracks.

Because Kyle was lying dead on the floor.

19.
Killer Comics

No matter how many times I see it, a pool of blood is a shock to my system.

I went into immediate emergency mode, phoning 911 and sending Joe to tell the super not to let anyone in or out of the building.

I stared down at Kyle. "Who did this to you?" I asked the corpse. None of our questions were going to be answered now.

I stood up super straight as it hit me. That might be exactly why Kyle got killed: to keep us from being able to question him.

Which meant we had to find a brand-new suspect— one who was willing to kill to keep this secret.

Once the police arrived, we wouldn't be allowed to search the studio. I had to move fast.

I wasn't going to take anything—I was just going to look. Honest. I know it's illegal to tamper with evidence.

I pulled my eyes away from Kyle and scanned the room. One quick look and I knew that the laptop was gone.

I carefully stepped around Kyle's body, making sure I didn't step into the pooling blood. My bloody footprints would just muck up the investigation. I flipped through an artist's portfolio.

Interesting. The sketches looked like preliminary studies for the *Dark Hawk* forgery. And the P. J. Rodriquez Ian had bought and returned.

It wasn't the kind of clue that would clinch the case with the police—or a grand jury. If asked, Kyle could have claimed the same thing Becky did—that he was just studying the art to improve his own skill. But the fact that the only drawings in this portfolio turned up as forgeries, well, that told me a different story.

"They're here," Joe announced, bursting into the room. I was so focused on Kyle and this new turn that I hadn't heard the sirens.

A moment later the building swarmed with cops.

A tall, thin police officer gave us a once-over. "What happened to you two?" he asked. "Have a run-in with the deceased and come here to settle up the score?"

Oops. I forgot about the fact that despite washing up, Joe and I still showed all the signs of the encounter with Kyle and his pals in Golden Gate Park.

The super stood at the top of the landing. "Those two boys were here earlier looking for Kyle."

He wasn't helping.

"Hey," Joe protested. "We were the ones who called this in! Why would we do that if we were involved?"

I turned to the super. "You saw us leave when we didn't find Kyle, right?"

The super shrugged. "I didn't see you come back. So I have no idea when you got here. I don't keep tabs on everyone coming and going."

A woman officer was taking notes. She looked up and asked, "Is there any kind of security camera?"

"Nope," the super answered.

"I'm surprised," I said. "The artists keep a lot of expensive stuff here." Now I looked the tall officer square in the eye, hoping that would take Joe and me off his suspect list. "I think this could be related to a burglary, sir. Kyle's laptop is missing."

Joe's mouth dropped. I wasn't sure if he was surprised by the fact that I had noticed that detail with a bloody body in the room, or by my giving the cops info—info that probably was linked to the case we were trying to solve ourselves.

I just wasn't ready to bring up the forgery, though. We didn't have concrete evidence, and these officers were already pretty suspicious of us. Besides, I really didn't want the cops all over Julia and the gallery as they investigated the murder. They might make it harder for us to complete the case for ATAC. If we could put the pieces together, then ATAC could take over—neat and tidy.

Somehow we managed to get the police to believe that we weren't involved. After giving them our contact numbers in case they had any more questions, we left.

"You thinking what I'm thinking?" Joe asked as we boarded the bus.

"About a long, hot bath?" I replied. My bruises felt like they were growing new bruises.

"That Kyle was making forgeries for someone else. And that someone else killed him to keep him quiet."

"Which means we're back to square one," I said. "Trying to figure out who is behind the forgeries."

"We do know something now that we didn't

151

before," said Joe. "We know that our criminal is willing to kill."

An hour later we were cleaned up and back at the convention. We were pretty certain it was the fact that we had been asking questions about the forgery that pushed the mastermind to kill Kyle. We might not have the absolute evidence needed at trial to prove that, but my gut knew it for sure. Joe's, too.

"So who knew that we were on this case?" I asked Joe, scanning the booths along Retail Row.

"Chet," Joe said.

I rolled my eyes. "Yeah, he's the one who put a bullet into Kyle."

Joe punched my arm. "No, dweeb. What I mean is that Chet may have accidentally spilled to someone."

I glared at Joe and rubbed my arm. "So not necessary." I'm no wuss, but I was still recovering from being whaled on by Kyle and his pal.

"Julia told P. J.," said Joe, ignoring my discomfort, "even though she wanted to keep it all quiet."

I glanced toward Julia's booth. P. J. was there again, signing autographs. "P. J. has no motive. Forgeries would devalue his work, not get him better deals."

"Jasper Scranton has known from the beginning," Joe pointed out.

"I just can't picture him shooting someone in cold blood."

"How many times has the bad guy turned out to be someone you'd never suspect?" Joe asked. "I think we should find out if he has an alibi."

My gaze wandered over to Clyde's Monsters and Heroes booth. "My money is on Fanelli," I said. "He's got a shady background and he has a lot to gain. And he's been talking to Kyle a lot lately."

"But I don't think he knew we were close to fingering Kyle as the forger," Joe said.

I shrugged. "Maybe he decided to get out of the game. The rumors were making it too dangerous, and so he got rid of Kyle."

"Possible," said Joe. "But none of this really feels right. The originals being switched but not turning up anywhere . . ."

"I know what you mean," I agreed, frustration welling up. "I feel as if we're missing something. Like we're not seeing the big picture."

Joe made a face. "Was that some kind of art forgery joke? 'Big picture.'"

I rolled my eyes. "That would be more your style. You're the one with the lousy sense of humor."

Ian rushed up to us, quite excited. "Oh, boys! Guess what I just bought!"

He held up a well-wrapped parcel. It was obviously some kind of artwork.

"A comic-book drawing?"

"The first drawing of Frank 'Fierce' Stone! And my very first Milner!"

"Julia must be thrilled," I said. "It helps prove that this gallery thing is really going to work."

Ian gazed lovingly at the brown paper as if he could see right through it to the image. "I can't wait to get this baby home!"

"I hope it works better than the P. J. Rodriquez," said Joe. "You don't want to have to return this one."

"Are you getting a chance to enjoy any of San Francisco aside from all the comic art?" Ian asked.

"Not really," I admitted. A brawl in Golden Gate Park did *not* qualify as enjoyment.

"It would be a shame if you spent all this time indoors," Ian said. "Tell you what—I've got a pair of Jet Skis just sitting there in the marina. They really should be used—just like my yacht."

"What do you think?" Joe asked me. I knew what he really meant: Could we take time off from the case to hit the water?

We could use the time on Ian's yacht to learn

a little more about the art world and collecting. Besides, it could clear our heads and inspire us to see the case with a fresh perspective.

Yeah. That's a good justification!

"Let's go for it!" I said.

Ian beamed. "Excellent. Come around seven. I'll be busy until then."

He gave us instructions on how to find his yacht at the marina, then trundled off with his pride and joy—the Milner.

"That'll be cool," Joe said.

I nodded. "And maybe we'll come back with a new idea!"

20.
Calling Card

The weather was perfect. The sun was low on the horizon, but it was still warm, and we'd probably have light for a little while longer—long enough to zoom those Jet Skis at least once around the bay at least.

Chet didn't join us. There was a special preview of the new movie starring Mercury. After that embarrassing incident when I interrupted the actors, the last movie I wanted to see was *that* one!

The salt on the breeze reminded me that the ocean wasn't too far away. But we were on the bay side, and once again the prison hunched on the island of Alcatraz, the sunset turning it pink and purple.

"Why is Alcatraz such a big deal?" I asked Frank

as we walked along the dock toward Ian's yacht.

"It was famous for being impossible to escape from," Frank explained. "Partly because the waters around here are so cold, and the currents so choppy."

"Maybe that's where our forger will do time," I said.

Frank laughed. "The place closed in the 1960s, bro. Do you think it would be a tourist attraction if it still held notorious criminals?"

Way to make me feel dumb. I guess I should have paid more attention when Frank and Chet read the guidebooks out loud on the flight here.

"This is it," Frank said, indicating a sweet vessel named *Collector*. Fitting for a guy like Ian. As promised, a pair of Jet Skis were tied to the back of the boat.

"He really must be rolling in the bucks," I commented, stepping aboard the luxury yacht. The wood gleamed, the brass shone, and every inch looked well cared for. This guy knew how to live.

"Mr. Huntington?" Frank called.

No response.

"Maybe he's down below?" I suggested. I found the steps leading below deck. "Could be giving instructions to the crew."

I took a few steps down. "Mr. Huntington?" I

called. Didn't want to surprise him getting changed into a swimsuit or anything. "It's us, Joe and Frank Hardy."

I found myself in a fancy lounge. A leather sofa, an armchair. An entertainment center.

And two framed comic-book drawings. The *Dark Hawk* cover and the P. J. Rodriguez.

I stared at them, trying to put it together.

I heard Frank behind me. "Isn't this the picture he returned?" I asked.

Frank looked puzzled too. "I thought so. But maybe it's a slightly different one from the same comic. I didn't get a really close look."

I stepped up to the *Dark Hawk* cover, a sinking feeling slowing my feet. That sinking feeling that comes from realizing you've been lured into a trap.

"Julia canceled the *Dark Hawk* cover auction because of the forgery," I said slowly. "So what is Ian doing with it?"

I turned and looked at my brother. His face was grim.

"The same reason Ian has this." He held up Kyle's very distinctive cell phone.

Ian was the man behind the forgeries.

21.

Mayhem at the Marina

"How did we miss this?" I exclaimed.

"Because there really weren't clear signs," said Joe. I knew he was as frustrated as I was that we hadn't thought of Ian up until now. "He was the guy *behind* the scenes."

"We were so focused on who did the actual forgery that we didn't look at anyone else."

"It all fits together now," Joe said, shaking his head. "Ian bought the original, had Kyle make the forgery, then brought back the fake."

"And while Kyle had the *Dark Hawk* cover in the shop for the frame job, he worked on that one. But he was more rushed, so he made a few mistakes."

"Hindsight is twenty-twenty," Joe said. "So now let's make this right."

A sudden lurching movement made me lose my balance. I stumbled into the drawings, knocking them over.

"We're underway!" Joe cried.

We raced to the stairs. I clambered up ahead of Joe—and found myself staring into the barrel of a revolver.

"Boys, boys, boys," Ian said. "Did you knock over my precious artwork? You really need to be more careful. The ones I have here are actually valuable."

I backed down the steps into the lounge. No good arguing with a guy holding a gun on you.

"You had to stick your noses in," Ian went on. "It was all going so well."

"You would have been caught sooner or later," I pointed out. "Julia and P. J. both knew about the forgeries."

"We just made sure you would be caught sooner," said Joe.

"What I don't understand," I said, buying time to try to come up with a plan, "is why go to all this trouble? You're obviously loaded. You can afford all the art you want."

Ian pursed his lips. "You'd think so, wouldn't you. But no. My money's tied up in all kinds of investments. More complicated than I would expect *you* to understand. But the cash flow gets limited when you have—" He broke off with a cough. "Well, when you enjoy taking financial risks now and then; some call it gambling, but . . . anyway, the point is that all this"—he gestured around the well-appointed lounge—"well, it's awfully expensive to keep up. And the art!" He made a little *tut-tut* sound.

"In the beginning, the comic art wasn't all that expensive. But its popularity made it skyrocket. And I just love it."

His eyes went to the drawings I had knocked over. I could see he was torn. He wanted to pick them up off the ground, but he didn't want to take his eyes—and gun—off us.

What if I tried to damage the drawings? That would freak him out long enough to get away.

Then again, I didn't think anyone would be very pleased if I destroyed the art we were trying to recover. And Ian would probably shoot me just for messing them up.

"It was such a brilliant solution," Ian said sadly. "I get my money back when I return the fakes, but I get to keep the wonderful originals."

He frowned. He looked like a little bald kid who'd just been told he had to put away his toys.

"If I had known that there was going to be so

much publicity around the *Dark Hawk* cover, I never would have had Kyle forge that piece."

"Why would you think Julia wouldn't make a big deal out of the *Dark Hawk*?" I asked. "It could put her on the map."

"Well, I know *that*," Ian said. "I just didn't realize it was going to go at auction. I planned to simply buy it myself. An auction is very risky."

Not as risky as being on an ATAC assignment, I thought.

"So what about Kyle?" Joe asked, obviously trying to stall Ian. "Why kill him?"

Ian snorted. "You must be able to figure out that one—to keep him quiet, of course."

Joe and I exchanged looks. Now what?

"Well, our time together is quickly coming to a close," said Ian.

"You're not going to get away with this," Joe said. "We told lots of people we were coming here."

That wasn't strictly true. We told exactly one person: Chet. But Ian didn't need to know that.

Ian just shrugged. "An old story—far too common. Reckless teenagers. Shouldn't be doing water sports at night and in such treacherous waters. . . ."

My blood chilled. He had it all worked out.

"Teenagers," Ian continued. "They just don't listen." He grinned. "It's really clever, isn't it? You go overboard, and no messy blood spoiling my beautiful yacht."

"Yeah," said Joe bitterly. "Don't want to get blood spatter on your precious comic-book drawings."

"You understand. Wonderful." Now Ian's gaze turned steely. He gestured with the gun. "Now up on deck. If I have to call the maid service to clean up your blood, I will."

I looked at Joe. Two of us. One of him. I liked the math.

Except a gun generally trumps addition.

We went above. The sun had gone down now, and we were far from shore. I guessed Ian had the boat on automatic pilot. I could see Alcatraz looming in the dusk.

Alcatraz prison might have been impossible to escape from, but I was determined that we'd somehow manage to escape from this.

Now that the sun was gone, it was chilly out on the water. I scanned the area—no other boats anywhere nearby.

This did not look good.

"Well, boys," Ian said, and not in a pleasant way, "time to say good-bye."

"Do we have to?" Joe asked. "I feel like we were only just getting to know each other."

"Enough jokes," growled Ian. "Jump. Now. Or I'll shoot you and toss you in myself."

If he shot us there was no hope. Not that there was a lot right now—but still . . .

I held up my hands to placate him. "Wouldn't want to ruin your fancy polished floors," I said.

"Now!" Ian ordered. "If you're still standing here when I reach three, I'm firing. One. Two."

Before he could get to three, we jumped.

Into the freezing, treacherous waters of the San Francisco Bay.

22.

Men Overboard!

What is it about this case and freezing cold water? This was the second time I'd wound up fully dressed in the bay.

Only I'd take the sea lions batting me around over Ian holding a gun on me any day.

I burst back up to the surface and gazed around, treading water. Where was Frank?

I spun in place.

Nothing. Not a ripple. Where was he? My heart sped up.

"Frank!" I shouted, kicking my feet and swirling my hands so that I'd stay above water. I had the all-too-familiar feeling of soaking wet clothes dragging me down. "Frank! Where are you?"

"Your brotherly love is touching," Ian sneered.

Anger warmed my freezing limbs. I splashed toward Ian. "You think you're going to get away with this? You're nuts. And how can you claim to love comic art when all you're dong is ripping off the artists?"

"Shut up, brat," Ian hissed.

"Oh, don't want to hear the truth, huh?" I knew I should be saving my strength—I had to stay alive— I had to somehow make it to shore, find Frank. But I couldn't help myself. This guy had my full fury.

"You are destroying everything you claim you care about!" I yelled. "Respect for the art. Stealing from the very people you say you admire."

And killing my brother! Blind rage gave me strength to stay afloat, despite the burning in my arms and legs, the tightness in my chest.

"I've had enough!" Ian raised the gun and pointed it straight at my head.

I ducked as he pulled the trigger. I straightened out and kicked hard, hoping that when I resurfaced it would be far enough away that he'd miss if he took a second shot.

I popped back up for air a moment before I felt my lungs bursting. The current had helped move the idling boat away, and I had a minute to regroup.

But there was still no sign of Frank.

Then a movement at the side of the boat caught my eye.

Frank! He hadn't drowned—he must have swum under the boat to the other side. While I was exchanging nasty words with Ian, Frank was sneaking onboard.

I knew what I had to do—keep Ian's attention long enough for Frank to get the upper hand.

"Ian!" I called. "Look, I'm still alive!"

Ian quickly turned toward me. "Not for long!" he shouted back.

That's what you think, sucker.

Frank crept up behind Ian and nailed him. A swift karate chop right to the sweet spot in the neck. Ian didn't have a chance. He crumpled to the deck.

Long, hard strokes brought me quickly to the boat. I scrambled up onto the deck where Frank stood over Ian. My brother held the gun straight at Ian's heart.

"Way to go, bro!" I cried.

"Help me tie him up," said Frank. "Then we can celebrate."

23.
Truly Original

"I can't believe how well the *Dark Hawk* cover did at auction!" Julia said.

We were at the PopCulture Gallery, celebrating the end of the convention. Not to mention wrapping up the case, recovering the stolen art, bringing Ian to justice, and Julia's phenomenal success repping the art she loved so much.

"I have to hand it to you," Jasper Scranton said, holding up a champagne glass to Julia. "I guess you do know a solid market when you see it."

"Thanks, Jasper," Julia replied. "I know it's not the kind of art you're into, so that means a lot."

"Just promise me one thing," said Jasper. "That there will always be room in our gallery for the work that I hold most dear."

"Of course," Julia said graciously. "There will always be a place for your paintings of Elvis Presley on velvet."

I choked on my sparkling apple cider. *That* was the kind of stuff Jasper considered art? He was one weird snob.

I gave Joe a look—it was time for our special presentation.

"Chet," I said as Joe disappeared into the storeroom. "We want to thank you for all of your patience. This was supposed to be your birthday present, and we spent a lot of time doing other things."

"That's okay," Chet said. "I know what you Hardys are like."

"Well, to make it up to you," I said, "Joe and I arranged for a special birthday present."

Joe came back in holding a framed drawing. P. J. Rodriquez followed him.

"An introduction to P. J. Rodriguez?" Chet said, his eyes wide.

"Even better," said Joe. He turned the picture around.

Chet's mouth dropped open, and he gasped.

I had to admit it—I was amazed myself. A little jealous, too.

"I wanted to do something special for the guys for helping us put an end to these forgeries," P. J.

told Chet. "But this was all they wanted. A drawing of mine—with you as the superhero!"

The drawing was a beaut. Full of trademark Rodriguez touches—tiny fairies in the foliage, strange creatures peering in from the borders. And in the middle of it all—a beaming comic version of Chet.

"And best of all," Joe said, "we know for a fact it's not a fake!"

The Hardy Boys are taking on a thrilling new case—so thrilling it will be a whole trilogy!

Check out a sneak peek at the first book of the new Hardy Boys Undercover Brothers Murder House trilogy,
Deprivation House.

FRANK

Ahh. A little downtime. Signing on as an agent with American Teens Against Crime (ATAC) is basically the coolest thing I've ever done. Knowing that I've helped bring in murderers and thieves and arsonists is a rush. Doing that with an organization my dad started up after he retired is even better.

But once in a while, it's good to be able to kick back in one of my favorite places—the school library. The biggest crime that's going to go down in here is somebody turning a book in late. And that's not my department.

Plus, I'm an information junkie, and this place has all the facts you need. If not in one of the books, then on one of the computers. I—

JOE

Joe here. You want to know the real reason Frank loves the library so much? It's because he's compulsively organized. I'm talking compulsive as in a psychiatric disorder. His label maker is one of his favorite things in the world. The library, with that whole Dewey decimal system to keep things in order, is paradise for him. Which is pretty pathetic. My paradise would have—

FRANK

Not in my section, Joe. Out. Anyway, as I was saying, I was hanging out in the library before first period, catching up on some homework. Joe was catching up on some z's.

My neurons started firing a little faster as I spotted a dark-haired guy pushing a cart full of books our way. Vijay Patel. There was only one reason for him to be at our school. We were about to get our next ATAC assignment.

I gave Joe a kick to wake him up. "You're Frank Hardy, right?" Vijay asked. He knows who I am. Vijay's been with ATAC almost as long as Joe and I have. He's one of the intel guys, but he's trying to get moved up to fieldwork.

"That's me," I answered.

"Here's the book you requested." Vijay slapped a bright blue book down in front of me, then rolled his cart away with a big grin on his face. I knew what the grin was about as soon as I read the book's title: *The Bonehead's Guide to Talking to Girls.*

Joe gave a snort-laugh. "You so need that."

Okay, so I sometimes have a tendency to blush when I'm talking to female types. But blushing is partially controlled by the automatic nervous system, although some volitional somatic control comes into play. So basically, a blush is not completely under the blusher's control. So I decided not to even answer Joe. Sometimes the best thing you can do with my younger brother is ignore him.

I cracked the cover of the book enough to see that the pages had been hollowed out. A game cartridge—our ATAC assignments always came in the form of game cartridges—some cash, and some ID and other background stuff were inside.

"Let's get out of here," I told Joe. He swung his backpack over one shoulder and followed me out of the library, through the quad, and out into the parking lot. I figured we could sit in the car and watch the "game" on Joe's portable player.

"Conrad at three o' clock," Joe warned me.

I adjusted the book Vijay had just given me so the title was absolutely hidden. If Brian Conrad saw it, I'd be hearing about it at least until graduation. So would everybody else at school. Including the girls I already had enough trouble talking to!

"Thanks," I said as I slid behind the wheel. I flipped Joe the game cartridge and he slid it into the player. We both stared at the blank screen expectantly. Hundred-dollar bills began to float from the top of the screen and land in piles at the bottom. To a *ka-ching, ka-ching* sound, a counter in the lower left tallied up the cash.

"Hello, Mr. Franklin." Joe let out a low whistle when the counter reached $1,000,000.

"*One million dollars could be yours—for living in this Mediterranean villa tucked up in exclusive Beverly Hills*," a woman's voice purred as the pile of money faded and was replaced by a photo of a mansion.

"Do you think there's a catch?" asked Joe. He scratched his head. "I'm thinkin' maybe there's a catch."

"Maybe one million dollars *could* be yours," I suggested, taking in the fountain out front, the palm trees, the balconies on all levels, the arched doorways, the red tile roofs. "Except there'd still be a catch. That place has to be worth multiple millions. I'm guessing double-digit millions."

"*Send us a tape showing us why you think you're special enough to compete. Teenagers only, please. And don't bother asking for more details. You won't get them.*" I could almost hear the woman smirking as she said that.

"Thousands of teens sent in tapes," the deep voice of our ATAC contact told us. Different views of the mansion flicked across the screen. A massive room with a fireplace big enough to walk into that I thought might be a living room. A home theater. A kitchen that looked like it belonged in a five-star restaurant.

"Twelve were chosen to live at the villa beginning this weekend," our contact continued. *"And at least one of the twelve has received a death threat."*

The screen blackened for a minute, then the *Gossip Tonight* logo flashed on. A film clip of a tall girl strutting down a red carpet started up. Short dress. Big smile.

"The list of people who want her dead has got to be pretty long," Joe commented.

"Why?" I asked. "And who is she anyway?" She looked sort of familiar. And she clearly had fans, but I couldn't come up with a name or what she had fans for.

"Ripley Lansing," Joe answered. He did his trademark my-big-brother-is-a-big-dork eye roll. "Her father's the drummer for Tubskull, and her mom owns some huge makeup company."

"Ripley Lansing received this letter yesterday," our contact went on, without emotion. A piece of deep red paper filled the game player's screen. Letters from different newspapers and magazines had

been glued on to form the message: "You win the $$$. You lose your life."

"Her parents have requested security at the highest level for Ms. Lansing, so the police have opted to bring in ATAC agents. Your mission is to go undercover as participants in the contest—details will not be available until you arrive at the villa—and find out who has threatened to kill Ms. Lansing. You will also need to determine if any of the other contestants are in danger."

The screen went blank and stayed blank. That was the only time we'd get our mission info. The cartridge erased itself after it was played once.

Joe picked up the book with the hollowed-out center and started flipping through the other stuff ATAC had sent us. "Tickets to L.A.," he said. "Cash." He raised his eyebrows. "You're not going to believe the cover story they came up with for us. It's like something out of a soap!"

He took a few more moments to scan the material. "Here's the deal. You and I are brothers."

"That *is* hard to believe," I commented. I reached over and brushed what I thought were some doughnut sprinkles off the front of Joe's shirt.

Joe ignored me. I guess that was only fair. "We got adopted by different families when we were babies," he explained. "We didn't even know about each other until a few months ago. I have really rich parents. Your family's more blue-collar."

"It's pretty extreme. Why do you think ATAC came up with something so out there?" I asked.

"Because they needed to get us on a reality TV show," Joe answered. "Those shows love extreme. Brothers separated as wee infants. One rich. One poor. I bet the producers ate that up with a spoon. I bet they think they'll get tons of drama out of us. Maybe they even think you'll try to beat me up—because I grew up with all the luxuries you never had."

"Have you ever considered the possibility that you watch too much TV?" I asked.

"Have you ever considered the possibility that you don't watch enough?" Joe shot back. "You didn't even know who Ripley Lansing is—and she's at the center of our case."

He had a point. "You said you thought there were a lot of people who would want her dead. Why?"

"So many reasons," Joe answered. "She's stolen boyfriends. She's gotten tons of people fired— everyone from waiters, to a backup singer in her dad's band, to an airline pilot. She's always breaking cameras when people try and take pictures of her. If we googled 'I want Ripley Lansing dead' we'd get enough suspects to keep us working for years."

"At least the note narrowed it down a little. The

person who wrote the death threat only wants Ripley dead if she wins the contest money," I reminded him.

"So I'm thinkin' that puts the other people in the contest at the top of the suspect list," said Joe.

"Whoever they are. And whatever the contest turns out to be." All missions start out with a lot of unknowns. But this one had more than usual.

Joe checked our plane tickets. "We'll find out tomorrow. We're flying out in the morning."

The first bell rang. "Right after school we need to strategize on what to tell Mom and Aunt Trudy," I said. Dad, of course, would already know the real deal, since he founded ATAC and everything.

I actually think Mom and Aunt Trudy would be cool with our missions. They'd worry about the danger, yeah. But they would get how important what we do is. They'd get that sometimes there are situations where teenagers are the best undercover operatives possible. But ATAC rules require absolute secrecy, so we have to keep Mom and Aunt T out of the loop.

"No can do," Joe answered. "Right after school I have to do a little shopping." He showed me the envelope full of cash from ATAC.

"Is there some special gear we need?" I asked.

"I'm going undercover as a rich boy. I need to look the part." Joe grinned. "The first piece of equipment I need is a pair of Diesel sunglasses."

I stared at him. "The ones you were drooling over at the mall? The ones that were almost three hundred dollars?"

"Authentic cover can make or break a mission, you know that." Joe slapped me on the shoulder. "Dude, those sunglasses could save our lives!"

"I don't think going on the show is a good idea, boys," Mom told us at dinner. "You've already missed a number of school days this year, and we're not even halfway through."

Mom always has the facts. Maybe it's because she spends so much time in libraries. She works in one, in the reference section.

"I agree," Aunt Trudy said. "Those shows are death traps. People have gotten burned, bitten by snakes. . . . I know someone lost a little toe, but I don't remember how. I'm sure that somebody is going to die on one of them soon, right in front of all the people watching at home."

"Aunt T, come on. All the contestants are teenagers. The producers are going to make extra sure everything we do is safe," Joe answered. "And it's me and Frank. You know we can take care of ourselves."

"Losers, losers, losers," Playback added from the kitchen. Our parrot seems to think he should have a part in every conversation. "Merry Christmas! Ho, ho, ho!"

Dad was the only one staying out of the discussion—for now. Joe and I are always telling him that we want to handle things ourselves, the way any other ATAC agents would have to. Agents whose father didn't start the agency. I think because we say that so much, sometimes he enjoys watching us sweat it out a little.

"Even if you don't die, they'll make you eat something horrible," Aunt Trudy went on. "Like worms. Then you'll come back with . . . with worms. Or parasites. Or some other nasty thing."

I looked over at Mom. "Can we go back to the school issue for a minute?"

She nodded.

"Joe and I have started designing an experiment around the experience of living in the house. We haven't worked out all the details, because we don't know what the specifics of the contest will be. We're definitely going to act as if we come from different socioeconomic backgrounds to see how that effects the judging. And we plan to come up with a few hypotheses on how the other people involved will behave under pressure." That last part was actually entirely true. "Our science and social studies teachers have given us the go-ahead to use the project to get class credit."

"And our English teachers are on board if we keep a journal every day and keep up on the reading. Plus we'll definitely get the assignments for everything else," Joe jumped in. "Even the principal thinks it's cool that the two of us could be on TV representing Bayport. Although we aren't exactly going to be ourselves. We're doing that socio-eco thing."

"I wish we knew more details," said Dad.

I couldn't decide if he was trying to make us sweat some more, or just trying to keep up his own cover of reasonable, concerned father who has no idea ATAC even exists.

"A million dollars could pay for lots o' college," Joe wheedled.

"True," Mom answered. She looked over at Dad. One of those looks that has a whole conversation in it. He gave a small nod. She gave in. "As long as you don't fall behind in school," she added.

"Great!" Joe was on his feet, gathering up dishes—even though no one had quite finished eating. "We're going to bring home the college money for sure," he said over his shoulder as he headed into the kitchen.

I picked up some empty plates and followed him. "You know we can't keep the money even if we win. We're not actually contestants. We're undercover," I reminded Joe, keeping my voice soft.

"Doesn't matter. It's only fair that if we win, we really get the money," Joe insisted.

"How do you figure?" I asked.

"Because if we get killed while we're under-cover, we're really going to be dead."

He had a point.

JOE

I adjusted my new sunglasses and stared at the huge wooden gate. Behind it lay the villa. I felt kind of like I'd stepped into the beginning of the Willy Wonka movie. A bunch of other kids and I were standing around waiting to be admitted into a sort of magical world.

I hadn't gotten a chance to suss out all the other golden-ticket holders yet. I'd shared a limo from the airport with my long-lost bro, Frank Dooley, a guy named Bobby T, and a girl who wouldn't say her name—or anything else. I'm talking not one word. Silent Girl just stared out the window the whole way here.

Bobby T talked enough for two people, though. He's a famous blogger. Well, he says he's famous. I've never heard of him. But he claims that World-view Pictures paid serious dough to option his blog so they could make a movie out of it. The option ran out before the movie got made, but he's hoping they'll renew the option and unload another dump truck of cash on him.

It looks like he's spent a big chunk of the cash he already got on hair product. For starters, his hair is mostly blue. And it stands out in all these different directions. It has a finger-in-a-light-socket thing going. That takes some serious mousse or pomade or gel. I know that from an undercover op.

FRANK

Frank here. The undercover op was as a student at Bayport High. His undercover identity: Joe Hardy.

JOE

Out, Frank.

Like I was saying, we were all standing in front of this massive gate. We couldn't see anything of the villa, because there was a wall around the place. While we were waiting for the gate to open, I noticed everybody kept shooting looks at Ripley Lansing. Even Frank—who barely knew who she was.

She was definitely worth looking at. She had super-straight, long, dark brown hair and ice blue eyes. And she had on a short dress, like the one in the clip that was part of our ATAC mission disk. Her legs were long and tan and basically awesome.

One of the guys I hadn't met pointed his camera phone at her. I was sure she was going to grab it and stomp on it, the way she supposedly did anytime anyone tried to take pictures of her.

Here it comes, I thought as I saw her hands clench and the muscles in her neck tighten. But then she tossed her hair and gave a big smile. Huh.

"It's opening," Frank said, pulling my attention away from Ripley. We all had to back up as the tall gate swung wide. A couple of cameramen circled around us to get our reactions as it did.

"Welcome!" a woman in a tight dark blue suit with matching dark blue shoes called out. Her hair was really blond, almost white, and her lipstick was very red. "I'm Veronica Wilmont, and I'll be your host—or maybe headmistress is a better term—while you're living here. I hope you'll consider me a friend, and—"

"I didn't come here to make friends," interrupted a wrestler-looking guy with a skull and crossbones shaved into the back of his short hair.

Veronica raised one eyebrow and looked at him. It was a look that could make icicles grow on your nose hairs. "James Sittenfeld," she finally said.

"That's me," the guy answered, throwing his arms wide.

"I remember your audition tape very well," Veronica told him. "I thought your so-called van-surfing was immature and incredibly dangerous—for yourself and for everyone on the road." She smoothed her already perfectly smooth hair. Her nails were very red too, and so wet-looking, I half expected the polish to wipe off in her hair. Not really, but you know what I mean.

"I didn't want you on the show, but I was overruled by the producers," Veronica continued. "They thought you'd be *entertaining*."

"I'll try to be entertaining when I crush everyone and walk away with the million." James winked at her. Veronica did not appear entertained.

This guy really wanted to win. But how bad? Bad enough to send Ripley that death threat?

PENDRAGON

Bobby Pendragon is a seemingly normal fourteen-year-old boy. He has a family, a home, and a possible new girlfriend. But something happens to Bobby that changes his life forever.

HE IS CHOSEN TO DETERMINE
THE COURSE OF HUMAN EXISTENCE.

Pulled away from the comfort of his family and suburban home, Bobby is launched into the middle of an immense, interdimensional conflict involving racial tensions, threatened ecosystems, and more. It's a journey of danger and discovery for Bobby, and his success or failure will do nothing less than determine the fate of the world. . . .

Coming Soon: Book Eight: *The Pilgrims of Rayne*

From Aladdin Paperbacks • Published by Simon & Schuster